T0381469

Watching myself through the window

La-Vern Johnson -Scott

authorHOUSE®

AuthorHouse™
1663 Liberty Drive
Bloomington, IN 47403
www.authorhouse.com
Phone: 833-262-8899

Published by AuthorHouse   10/16/2024

ISBN: 979-8-8230-3396-1 (sc)
ISBN: 979-8-8230-3004-5 (e)

Library of Congress Control Number: 2024919380

Print information available on the last page.

DEDICATION

. . . .

To my children Bryan and Omeka, I have been the honey
and vinegar in your lives. I hope that you carry it with you
because you will have the bitterness and sweetness in life.
I love you both more than you know.

Acknowledgements To my SWR SISTERS,

Jewel Scott, Brenda Brown, Marie Wilder, Shelia Bailey
thank you for your love, and your encouragement during
this journey.

CONTENTS

· ·

INTRODUCTION

All of my children are special, but my girls and I have a special bond. My girls inherit a gift as I did from the old African woman. We can only discuss this gift with each other or other female family members that acknowledge their gift. They are the only ones that understand and don't think we are crazy. The love of a man to lure her away from her village, she was captured by slave hunters who endured the voyage across the Atlantic Ocean and entered this country in Charleston, S.C., in the early 1800's. Out of fear she could not speak in her native tongue, speak her African name, or practice her gift; everything that came from Africa was evil according to the slave owners. Many family members choose to use their gift, and others decide to turn away from it. Generations of Christianity made our gift evil, or you were worshipping the devil. My mother was one who decided not to use her gift she inherited and told my sister and I we should not because it was the devil's work. My aunt, Big Ma, taught me how to use my gift without my mother's knowledge because I was such a natural. I never revealed my Big Ma's teachings to my mother out of fear that she would stop me from spending time with her. When my girls started to recognize their differences, I explained to them that their inheritance was a gift, similar to many other women in my family, but the choice of how or whether to use it rested with them. When they were old enough to help me in the kitchen, I started teaching them the things that Big Ma taught me. I clarify that we keep this a secret and advise them not to share their gift with others, as they don't want to face judgment or embarrassment from those who lack understanding. As they got older, I told them if they chose to abandon their gift, that's fine with me. I would never force it on them. Like Sarah, many chose the love of a man and disregarded their special gift, which warned them that the man they chose to love would use, hurt, harm, and endanger their lives. Sarah's path was followed by generations of women in my family. It occurred to my big mama, my daughter, and myself. Watching what happened was like watching myself through the window.

CHAPTER 1

Family

A MOTHER KNOWS HER CHILDREN. I MAY NOT KNOW THE EXACT situation, but I have intuition that has not failed me in my fifty-two years. I have a good relationship with all of my children. They received punishments and sometimes got their behinds whipped.

They were your typical children, but for the last eighteen years, I had to be stern because I had to be both mother and father. One of the demands was that they were to complete high school and, if desired, pursue a college education, and beyond if they chose too. They all accelerated in their academics, and I insisted that they take up vocational training in auto mechanics, so they had some knowledge and skills in how an automobile runs.

I was blessed. Five of my six children had college degrees. My second child Shauna Allie was born with developmental challenges. When she was born, she was our gift from God. Her siblings treated her no different. They refrained from insulting her or permitting others to do so due to her uniqueness. Shauna engages in activities similar to those of her siblings. While she may not engage in the same activities as her siblings, it is not due to a lack of effort on her part. She was employed until the pandemic closed everything, and now, year one into this pandemic, nothing much has changed. Shauna has received instruction in individual living skills and is also responsible for household chores. Her siblings pay her to fold their clothes and put them outside their door. Shauna assists Lois and me in the kitchen by rinsing off the dishes before I put them in the dishwasher and she wipes down the stove, table, and counter. Shauna's employment situation has remained stagnant since the start of the pandemic, but she continues to contribute at home by helping with chores and learning important life skills. Despite the challenges she faces, Shauna remains proactive and engaged in her daily activities.

I gave all my children the same speech. Unless they received a full scholarship, they were forced to attend a state college due to other considerations. I would cover the cost of an undergraduate degree, but they would be responsible for funding their further education. That all changed. All six played basketball in high school and college. Lillian and Bella played softball. Shauna played basketball for the Special Olympics.

They all attended my alma mater, Virginia Central College. Raymond Howard was a high school basketball coach, and after receiving his master's, he was a guidance counselor. Ernest Fredrick was a computer specialist and entrepreneur who had his own store selling new and used computers. His business was still doing well. Due to the pandemic, he closed his store, sold only online, and worked at home repairing computers. He created a program for Shauna, collaborated with her, and taught Gerald how to assist her.

Ernest Fredrick had a twin sister, Bella Rose, who was three minutes younger. Bella Rose, a licensed mental health therapist and hair stylist, has transitioned from her original shop.

During the pandemic, Bella Rose was selling lace front wigs online. Bella Rose has always had a passion for helping others feel confident and beautiful, which is why she decided to combine her skills in therapy and hairstyling to offer virtual consultations for wig customization. This new venture allows her to reach a wider audience and continue supporting her clients' mental health and self-esteem.

My baby boy, Gerald Louis, was My godly man, who holds an undergraduate degree in finance, has recently completed his master's degree in divinity and has been ordained as a minister. He's my stock market person. Even though he's younger than Shauna, he's her father figure. Gerald Louis was always a guiding light for Shauna, providing her with wisdom and support beyond his years. Love and respect for one another have strengthened their unbreakable bond.

Lillian Sade, my baby, was an actress and drama queen who had minor roles in various movies. In her last three films, she portrayed a prominent female character, and her most recent film garnered significant commercial success. Lilian clung to me more than any of my other children. The only times she did not live at home were in college, on Broadway, or filming a motion picture. During those times, she would secure a hotel suite for herself, a practice she continued until it concluded. Despite her success in the industry, Lillian always valued family above all else and made sure to stay connected with us no matter where her career took her. Her dedication to both her craft and her loved ones was truly admirable.

I have six grandchildren. My oldest son Raymond is a single father, and he has a son named Blake. My twin Ernest married his college sweetheart, Trudy, and has a daughter named Ella. Bella has a daughter named Anya and a son named Isaiah. Bella divorced her husband after having her daughter. He has never seen her. Lillian just had twins, a boy Zachery, and a daughter Zanna.

CHAPTER 2

. . . .

COVID 2020

WE ARE LIVING THROUGH A COVID PANDEMIC. WE PROHIBIT anyone who does not reside here from entering our property. I lived on a forty-thousand-acre estate with an eight-foot electronic fence and backup generators.

When the country went into lockdown, I met with all my staff. I explained the situation and the necessary actions everyone should take to prevent the virus from spreading. I explained to my staff there was no cure for a virus. Every day, thousands of people died.

1. They were required to reside in staff housing on the property.
2. You are not allowed to leave without informing the head of staff, Lois.
3. They would have to spend ten days in quarantine if they had to leave the property before they could return.
4. No one from outside the property could visit them.

Lois was my right-hand, and she was more like family since she had been my nanny and housekeeper when I got pregnant with the twins. Every morning at eight, we met to go over the agenda for the day, which included building, grounds, meals, children/grands and appointments. I worked with my property management team from nine to ten in the morning. Yes, I owned property. I bought houses, renovated them, and rented them only to those who received Section eight. Poor people needed nice places to live, too. In the years of renting houses, I never evicted anyone.

All of my property management employees worked from home. They all were single parents with young children. They all rented houses from me. The ancestors instructed me to prepare this oil, placing the cross of Jesus at each entrance, and ensuring there was enough for my entire family to use in each house. Each vehicle had hand sanitizer and a mask to use if they went to the store, and we all had to wear a mask when we left the property.

CHAPTER 3

. . . .

Christmas 2020

IT WAS CHRISTMAS TIME. WE HAD DECORATED THE HOUSE since the day after Thanksgiving. The cooks received the Christmas menu a month in advance. For everyone, Christmas Eve dinner was a seafood boil. After eating seafood and everyone cleaned up, we would sing carols, play cards and board games, and just have fun. We included all staff members who lived on the property, just as we did last year. Every staff member received a breakfast invitation on Christmas Day, during which they exchanged gifts with each other. We would all have dinner together around four.

Lillie was the only one who didn't have to spend time in quarantine; while filming her last movie, they lived in quarantine. She had flown home in a private jet with the film director, who dropped her off, and she tested negative when she got off the plane.

Because she stayed in her suite the majority of the time, I thought she was tired. There was something different about Lillie when she returned. Her favorite time of year was always Christmas. However, this time she seemed distant and preoccupied. A quiet demeanor replaced her usual bubbly and talkative nature. When Lillie returned home before the holidays, she would go and check out the decorations, inside and outside. She would shake the boxes with her name on them trying to guess what her siblings intended to give her. However, this time she appeared distant and unresponsive. It was clear that something had changed within her during her time away.

She interacted, but not like she normally would. There was no happiness in her eyes anymore. The only time I saw her smile was when she got a phone call, and then she would leave the room to continue her conversation in private. On Christmas Eve, she received twenty-five beautiful red roses and a diamond tennis bracelet. She did not tell us who she received the gifts from, and no one asked her either. Lillie was very close to Trudy and Bella. While cleaning after Christmas dinner, the question came up, "What was going on with her?" and "who sent the gifts?". No one knew.

Tonight, after dinner, we decided to watch her new movie. When she returned home, she had a copy of the DVD, for family only. They filmed the movie in New Orleans. It was positive about relationships, and in today's society, you can't take anything for granted.

As I watched the movie, I focused on her, and when they got to the second love scene, I knew. My baby was in love. Although my child was an exceptional actress, I am aware that this was a genuine expression of her emotions.

When she first talked to me about auditioning for this movie, she told me who her leading man was, Jacoby Sessoms. "I advised her to pursue it, but keep in mind that

Jacoby Sessoms is a ladies' man, so it's important not to mix emotions." I was leery about it. Jacoby Sessoms was not a negative person; he had starred in many movies, produced, and directed. Women gravitated towards him due to his attractiveness, with the majority of his past girlfriends were of different nationalities.

Many rumors suggested that his current relationship was fake, as he was attempting to improve his image by dating more women of color. His current girlfriend, Shelly, has dated numerous athletes and actors with less than stellar reputations. His current girlfriend hails from a wealthy entertainment family. Every tabloid, internet, and talk show featured photos of them together. Whenever Jacoby or her father Thomas appeared on any show, there was constant discussion about their relationship with Shelly. I was really concerned, but I stayed out of my children's business once they became adults; I only gave my opinion when they asked me. I was not that controlling, like my mother was.

CHAPTER 4

I Am Changing 1979

THIS IS THE FIRST CHRISTMAS THAT I HAD TO TRAVEL HOME; it felt good because if I did not feel like putting up with any foolishness, I could always pack up and return to my own apartment. My parents got on my damn nerves, but I loved them to the moon and back. We all left our homes, departed from the city, and three of our four children left the state. We all decided to go home for the holiday because our younger brother had returned from a three-year tour duty in Germany.

I moved to Northern Virginia in July and have not returned since I moved. I resigned from my old school division because they were not progressive enough. I am now able to fully utilize my skills and passion for teaching in a more supportive and innovative environment. The change has been refreshing, and I am excited to continue growing in my new role. I loved my new teaching position. I look forward to going to work daily as a language specialist.

The weekend prior, I went with my roommate to her Christmas party in D.C. She worked as an interpreter for the United Nations. The hotel was beautifully decorated. There were delicious foods from different countries. The music and the atmosphere were nice. I really enjoying myself. There were people there I knew and connected with some nice individuals.

Returning from the restroom, a gentleman bumped into me; we both said, "Excuse me," and I continued to my table. Someone said, "Keep walking." The ancestors reminded you constantly they were there and would speak to you when they saw trouble. I simply ignored the person who was staring at me every time I turned my head. Finally, he approached and asked me to dance, and I replied yes. We exchanged names during our couple of dances and engaged in a conversation about how we had arrived at this party. I returned to my table, and the couple that was sitting next to me left for the night.

Once he realized the couple had left for the night, he approached the table and asked, "Can I sit? and everyone replied, ""Yeah." We exchanged small talk for the remainder of the night. When Gwen and I decided to leave, he asked me if he could have my phone number, and I said "yes." He recorded my phone number in a small book he had on the inside of his tux jacket. After that, he tore out a sheet, wrote his name and number on it, and asked me to give him a call. I closed the paper in my purse and bid everyone goodnight.

The following Thursday evening, my phone rang, and the voice on the other end asked, "Did you forget me that quick?" My reply was, "Who am I forgetting?" "It's me; remember we met at the Christmas ball, Philip Fontenot?"" I thought I would hear from you by now". I explained to him that "my mind was on preparing to close for the holidays, going home, etc." He started explaining to me that he was getting ready to travel to Louisiana for a two-week stay. He shared details about his large family, being the seventh of twelve children, his graduation from Texas State College in business administration, his role as a commission officer in the Marines, and his Creole heritage from Lake Charles, Louisiana.

This was a big turn-off for me, especially when he began to talk about his Creole heritage. On the east coast, we encountered a similar group of individuals who did not identify as Creoles yet shared a common mindset. They only married individuals who resembled them, ensuring that their light skin would continue into the next generation. My own grandmother was similar to this, but she married a brown-skinned man, with some of her children being light-skinned and others being brown. She treated my papa like dirt and never bonded with her browner grandchildren, especially me. She never showed me the same love and affection as she did for my lighter-skinned cousins.

He asked me to meet him for lunch on Saturday, and I said yes. I really was not interested because all he talked about was himself. If he thought I was impressed by his looks, he was wrong. Attractive, yes, but I learned long ago there was more to a person than their looks.

We ordered lunch and talked about what we were doing during the two weeks off. He stated that he would be spending the whole two weeks at home. He only had the opportunity to visit his family twice a year, and each visit lasted for two weeks. This time he planned to spend as much time with his grandmother; she was almost 95 years old. Her health was very frail. He called her grand mere.

He inquired about my grandparents, to which I replied that I had a shared birthday with my maternal grandfather, who passed away before my birth, and my grandmother, who passed away when I was seven years old. Although my paternal grandmother and I did not have a relationship, we shared a deep love for my Papa, both of whom had passed away. He explained to me that the majority of his family spoke French and English, but among each other they only spoke French. Then he said, "When I take you home, I don't want you to feel left out, not understanding the language."

When I began to speak French, he looked puzzled. I explained that I was a language specialist instructor, and I had spent one summer in Haiti, one summer in France, and one summer in Cuba, so don't let this southern accent fool you.

I asked him, "Where did he get the idea I was going to Louisiana?" He asked for my parent's phone number, hoping to call me during the holiday. I gave him the number and informed him that I had to leave because I had made plans with some friends. He asked me, "Can I kiss you?" "Sure", I responded by allowing him to kiss me on the cheek. The ancestors came that night while I slept and said, "stay away from him."

He called me a couple of times, but I wasn't there. I asked my parents if he had left a number, and finally he did. We spoke four times during the holiday. What really annoyed me was that when we were on the phone, he would be carrying on a conversation with someone else in French. I told him to call me back, but don't try to multitask two conversations at once

13

CHAPTER 5

Inheritance 1979

MY PARENTS, JACOB AND ELIZA MCCRAY, HAD BEEN MARRIED for forty-one years. Daddy was a functional alcoholic who gambled and pursued any skirt he could find, while Mama was a strict, Bible-beating licensed practical nurse. They were both natives of North Carolina. Daddy grew up as a sharecropper, but Mama's family-owned land that she grew up on. Their family farm grew cotton and tobacco, but the wealth was shared among family members.

At the age of ten, Papa needed Daddy's help picking cotton, prompting him to drop out of school, while Mama successfully completed her high school education. Mama moved to Virginia with her sister and went to night school to get her nurse's license. Daddy worked in the shipyard from the age of eighteen; he loved the job but hated the daily racism that all blacks dealt with. When he was drunk, his favorite saying was, "Get your education; knowledge can't be taken away."

Mama took her vows seriously. When Daddy would come home drunk and want to argue, Mama would never back down. Instead, she'd speak her mind and tell him to carry his drunken ass to bed. Nobody is going to argue with your drunken asses tonight. My older siblings were unable to cope with the situation; as soon as they graduated from undergrad, they secured jobs outside the state and pursued graduate school. My youngest brother chose to join the military instead of attending college. I was the only one who came back home after college. One Saturday night, amidst Daddy's arguments and drunkenness. I spoke with Mama. Why did she continue to tolerate this behavior? Just leave!. You don't have any small children; all you have is yourself." As a devout woman, Mama affirmed, "There is only one perfect person, and that's Jesus. When I stood before the minister and God, I truly meant what I said, for better or worse. You're unaware of the struggles your father endures in this life. He is an uneducated black man. Because of the hardships your father faces outside the house, you, your brother, and your sister have been able to receive a college education. Additionally, you have grown up in a well-established neighborhood where no one has ever gone hungry. No one has ever turned off our electricity, gas, or water. Your daddy brings me his check every week." I said, "But mama, he has affairs with other women," to which she responded, "They don't get much, that I know." Furthermore, he doesn't have anything to give them because I get the check and the check stub, so I know how much money he keeps for himself. I love the man regardless.".

When I visited Big Mama one night, she noticed that I was troubled about something and asked, "What's on your mind, child?" I told her about the previous conversation with Mama, to which she replied, "Your mother received a warning." The ancestors will always warn you if you are heading in the wrong direction, particularly if the man you are loving is the source of your hurt and pain. Those of us with the gift choose to stay in hell or get out. Staying in a marriage that is challenging makes you stronger regardless of what happens.

Your mama is a strong woman, but life has made her a bitter woman." When I questioned her about her husband, her response was, "Like all I was warned." I never allowed my husband's erratic behavior to bother me. His constant mischief led to his death at the hands of this woman's husband. "How long were you married, I asked?" "Two years she answered." "Why did you not remarry?" I asked. With tears in her eyes, Big Mama responded, "I chose to live my life in peace." Every man I tried to love was devious in some form or fashion, and I got sick of the old souls riding my back."

Each of us had been working for years. Jacob Jr. was an accountant for Georgia State. He married Chelsie, and they had three children. My sister Carol lived in Durham, N.C., married to her high school sweetheart Jason. They too had three children. My younger brother Wiley, who was not married, had a son; I was single and had no children. I was content with my life, focusing on my career and traveling the world.

. Daddy would always tell us that when he died, he only left enough to take care of Mama, but this time he told us he had won fifty thousand acres of land in a card game. He wanted to give each of us 1000 acres a piece. We looked at Mama, and she stated it was legit. Mama took out the deed to the land, and Jacob Jr. looked over it and said it was legal. We rode up to the city's outskirts, and there it was. After we returned to our parents' home, we sat at the dining table and discussed the land and paying taxes.

All my siblings backed out due to financial constraints; they had already purchased homes and had no intention of moving back to Virginia. I thought to myself, "Damn, I'm going to have to take care of my parents when they can't take care of themselves," but I didn't mind because I love them so much. I was not surprised; I have been taking care of my parents for the majority of my adult life. Daddy signed the deed in my name, and every month, I deposit money into an account in my father's name, ensuring we have the necessary funds for the six-monthly tax payments. I cautioned Daddy not to force me to return home to retrieve my money, as I am sure I will.

CHAPTER 6

. . . .

Opening Up 2021

I HAD A DOCTOR'S APPOINTMENT THE MONDAY FOLLOWING THE Christmas holidays, and as I was getting out of the shower, Lillie tapped on my door and asked where I was going. I told her I had a doctor's appointment and she asked, Could she go? I said yes, and she said she would drive.

Once we were in the car out of earshot of anyone, her feelings began to pour out like rain. The upscale hotel they were staying in was their home. You needed a badge to enter their floor; Jacoby's suite was across the hall from hers. Some nights, they would eat together, play board games, cards, or just watch movies or TV shows. They got to know each other well because they discussed their personal lives. They discussed family traditions, their upbringing, and their likes and dislikes during their conversation.

The subject of Shelly never came up. In the first love scene, I was with Jacoby. I knew I had feelings for him, but by the time the second love scene came, she confessed that she was developing feelings for him, and he could sense it. I have seen many of her movies. Even the kisses she shared with her leading men didn't hold the same significance as those in this particular movie. Lillian expressed uncertainty about whether he harbored feelings for her or was aware of her developing feelings for him. He stopped coming over to her room, so she kept her distance. I said, "The movie never showed any tension between them." I asked her, "Did she ask him why the change in attitude, Lillian?"

The red-carpet movie preview night was a momentous occasion. I was hesitant to attend because I had to use a wheelchair. When she started talking to me about attending, I informed her of my hesitation. Lillian said, Mama, I will never feel embarrassed about you having to use a wheelchair. I would remain proud of you out of love for you, even if you were compelled to use a backward donkey.

As they introduced the movie's stars, I observed their interaction, revealing a hint of sparks. A glow emanated from their faces. It brought me back to a time in our lives when her father and I were together.

After that, we went to dinner. Jacoby introduced his parents, Jennifer and Lynell, to me. They were beautiful, spirited people, and I was delighted to get to know them. Jennifer and I exchanged numbers and promised to stay in touch and visit when we could travel safely.

Lillian continued, "After saying our goodbyes to everyone, I returned to my hotel suite and there was a knock at my door. I asked who it was, and when he said Jacoby, I opened the door so he could enter. As I turned to return to the couch, he grabbed me by the wrist, pulled me in, and kissed me passionately. I returned the kiss because I so missed him and his presence in my life. Jacoby began to tell me the reason he had stayed away from me the past two weeks. He wanted to confirm his feelings for me. He admitted that his relationship with Shelly had come to an end. Jacoby was a private person, and he wanted to keep it that way. Shelly frequently shared photos of them together. He requested that Shelly refrain from posting the photos. Shelly said that she was not posting them; it was her publisher.

An article about the impending nuptial made headlines. They quoted her father as saying he would be delighted about their marriage; he understood it would terminate their relationship, as he would not submit to coercion into marriage. He said that his heart was leaning in another direction. He could no longer lie to himself.

That night I laid in his arms and slept better than I had slept in a long time. Lillie continued to say, "Mama, we did not have sex, so get your mind out of the gutter. Mama, I apologized profusely for her snobbish behavior during the holidays. I miss him so much.

I asked, "Where did he go for the holidays?" Lillian replied, "He went home to California to be with his parents for the holidays. His next movie is scheduled to take place in Atlanta. Would it be possible for him to spend some time with me before entering quarantine to prepare for his next movie? Of course I replied, "But he will need a negative COVID test before he enters the grounds." Lillie looks at me and smiles, then she says, "Mama, I have never fallen in love before, but I am now."

While sitting in the doctor's office, I texted Bella and told her I needed to spend time with my girls tonight, and after dinner, I needed her, Lillian, and Shauna to come up to my suite. I knew that Shauna was protected by the ancestors. One night, when I went to check on her before bed, I heard her talking to the ancestors, naming them Hattie, Essie, Sarah, and Tilda.

That night we were in my suite. I asked Bella and Lillian, Do the ancestors ever come to you?" Bella began to tear up and said they used to fuss at me all the time, especially during my teen years, when I thought I was getting away with something. Bella never mentioned her ex-husband by name, but she said she knew he was not the one because the ancestors told her to beware of him numerous times. The night before my marriage, as I fell asleep, the ancestors appeared to me in a dream, warning me that the bed I made would be the bed I would have to sleep in until I found relief from my misery. Lillian informed me that her ancestors had provided her with information about some of the men she had dated. She would not date them again out of fear. I asked her if they had approached her about Jacoby; she replied that they hadn't, but they had warned her about Shelly's attempts to tarnish her image. Both of my daughters inquired whether I had received any warnings, to which I replied in the affirmative. They simultaneously inquired about their father, to which I responded in the affirmative. I have no remorse for the decision, as I have been blessed with six beautiful children.

CHAPTER 7

....

1980 Family

PHILIP AND I HAD BECOME EXCLUSIVE. WE SPENT A LOT OF time together, and I realized we had a lot in common. We were both football and basketball fans; we enjoyed recreational sports like kickball, tennis, and table tennis, and we both loved the beach. We also enjoyed attending concerts. When we weren't working, I loved wearing jeans and pulling my hair up in big curly puffs. My hair was naturally curly, and I never used any chemicals, but on special occasions, I would occasionally straighten it. He would attend after-school affairs with me. With him, I would attend military dinners, ceremonies, and military balls.

Philip stood out in many ways; he was attentive, he could read my face and knew when I was having a rough day at work. He would cook, and he would rub my feet, a gesture I was ashamed of because I had bunions. He would take me out to dinner at foreign restaurants. He knew I loved Cuban and Jamaican foods, and he would call in orders, pick them up, and bring them home for dinner.

There never had to be an occasion for him to send me flowers. Every year during my spring break, we would take trips to different Caribbean islands. He loved me, and he always showed public displays of affection.

I learned a lot about his personal life. He followed his two older brothers into ROTC at college to alleviate his parents' financial burdens, as he still had siblings at home. He also gained significant insight into my personal life. I had problems with trusting people. Prior to meeting him, I was in two relationships. My high school boyfriend cheated on me with my best friend and got her pregnant. The guy I dated in college was promiscuous and slept with anyone who entertained him; I also witnessed my dad engaging in numerous affairs with my mother. Philip acknowledged his understanding, assured me he wouldn't conceal anything, and demonstrated his transparency.

He informed me about the Mardi Gras celebration at his brother's house. Many of his Louisiana friends were at sea and couldn't participate. He asked if I would be interested in attending and meeting some of his family and friends. I agreed because it would give me a chance to see my parents, whom I hadn't seen since the Christmas holidays. We decided to depart that Friday night and secured a hotel room in Hampton. He made reservations at the Va. Beach hotel; his brother and his wife were staying there. I did not feel comfortable staying with any family at the moment.

I made a phone call to my parents on Saturday morning, and when I arrived, Mama had prepared a light brunch for us. I introduced Philip to my parents. Naturally, my mother asked numerous questions, but we quickly left after our meal.

When we arrived at his brother's house, I was surprised by the number of people inside. In the backyard, there were two-gallon grills cooking food, and there were about four cookers with seafood boils going. Everyone was from a different part of Louisiana, and some of them spoke French or had a distinct Louisiana dialect.

. When we entered the house, Philip started looking for his brothers; when they saw him, they both rushed over, hugged, and got their wives attention. I was shocked at how much they looked alike; I thought I was looking at triplets. The oldest of the three was Lamont; he was four years older than Philip, and he married his high school sweetheart, Cheryl, and they had two children. The next was Donnell, who was two years older than Philip. He met and married a young lady from North Carolina, Jessica, and they have a six-month-old. Despite Cheryl's cordial demeanor, she was deeply engrossed in a conversation with her homegirl, Lashay Baptiste, and if appearances could kill, I would be dead.

Finally, Lashay walks over and introduces herself, stating that she is the cousin of his last girlfriend and best friend. I said, "Nice to meet you, Lashay; my name is Charlotte, and I am Philip's current girlfriend." Jessica loved it and said you are going to marry Philip. I explained to her we had only been dating for four months, and that's the last thing on my mind. We will continue to talk and observe.

Jessica began to tell me that everyone thought that Philip and Suzanne were going to get married, but she broke off their relationship after he followed his brothers in ROTC and went active duty. She was aware that three of the

Fontenot children were enrolled in college concurrently, and they made the necessary arrangements to alleviate their parents' financial burden, given the presence of other children at home. Suzanne hails from a wealthy family, accustomed to demanding her own terms. Although her father was willing to contribute, he chose not to assume any responsibility toward Suzanne's father.

Suzanne was visiting his parents during the Christmas holidays and told him that she wanted them to get back together. He responded that too much time had passed and he felt it was best for her to move on. Since then, he has not had a steady girlfriend. Now he is no saint; he's dated, and he told his brothers about you when he was home for Christmas. Philip finally found me among the crowd and put his hands around my waist as I stood there talking to Jessica. Finally, she asked me if I was going down south for Juneteenth. Philip mentioned it to me, but I have not given an answer. Jessica says girl, come on and go; we will have a fun time. We can hang with each other.

I can give you the information you need to know. When we return after two weeks, you can celebrate the Fourth of July with your parents. Remember, your parents mentioned that all your siblings would be at home, so I said, "Okay, that sounds good." Staying two weeks is no problem; I do not have any classes or workshops to attend this summer. There was a lot of eating and drinking, so we caught a cab to the hotel. Donnell and Jessica had reservations at the same hotel and Lamont picked us up. We had brunch, and they gave us food for the road. We hugged and said our goodbyes. I went by and spent a couple of hours with my parents.

I drew my mother aside to discuss the Fourth of July celebration. I inquired if it would be acceptable to invite Philip's two brothers and their families. She agreed, and I informed her that I would be traveling to Louisiana for the Juneteenth celebration. We planned to return at the end of June, and I promised to help her as soon as I got back.

CHAPTER 8

························

Intimacy 1980

I HAD NO EXPERIENCE WITH INTIMACY OR SEX. NO, I WASN'T A virgin; I surrendered my virginity to a boyfriend in college. I felt very insecure when I was with him. He would constantly point out flaws in my appearance. Despite my shape, I had to learn from my friends how to choose clothes that accentuated my body, as I was accustomed to dressing like a potato sack. I ended up giving all my larger clothes to some of the girls that could wear them, and when that happened, I started to get attention from guys on campus.

The night I met Philip, I had on a gown that didn't show my assets. My attitude was that if I had to attend a formal affair, at least be comfortable. When I saw Philip the next time, I wore a pair of not-too-tight jeans and a hoodie. I had to give my sister girl room to breathe, and he was shocked. He couldn't take his eyes off those assets, which I reminded him of during our holiday conversation. Talk to me, not my chest or my ass. He told me that he was shocked that I had such a beautiful figure, and why would I try to hide it?

I knew this man would be a steady force in my life, so I made an appointment with my gynecological doctor for birth control pills. I made a quick trip home to get a pap smear and my prescription, but I always carried doubts because you never know what might happen. After about three months of dating exclusively, we became intimate.

We had spent many nights together, but there was no sexual contact. We slept in the same bed, and he began to slowly seduce me. On some nights, he would simply embrace me, reassuring me of his unwavering protection.

Some nights he would just kiss me. He would kiss me so intensely that I would have to catch my breath, and he would comfort me by saying, "Breathe, baby." On some nights, he would caress and massage areas that I had no idea were so sensitive, causing me to relax and yearn for more affection. While getting me prepared, he taught me how to touch him to make him feel as good as I felt.

The night we first made love, he ran a bath for me and slowly bathed me. Once finished and towel-dried, he rubbed me down with a cream that smelled like strawberry cake and made your skin shine like new money. He started kissing me and instructed me to turn onto my stomach. Using his tongue, he slid it from the base of my neck all the way down my spine to my buttocks, a sensation that sent chills throughout my entire body. He gently turned me over and began to kiss me, gently cupping each breast as his hand slid down between my thighs, slowly opening them. He began to rub the inside of my thighs up to my vagina and began to slowly rub my erotic button, my back arch wanting more. He ascended onto me, aware that it had been more than three years since I had sex. He gradually penetrated me, a small amount at a time, until he was fully ensconced and my body welcomed him. Our bodies slowly moved in unison with each other, until we could no longer resist. We lay in silence, our bodies drenched in beads of sweat. The ancestors whispered in my ear as I lay in his arms, "You didn't listen to our warning".

CHAPTER 9

· ·

Juneteenth 1980

SCHOOL WILL BE CLOSING IN A COUPLE OF DAYS, AND SOON I will journey to Louisiana to meet Philip's family. Jessica called me one night at my apartment and asked me," Can you talk?"" I said yes." She started by saying, "I want to give you a heads-up about what you are walking into.

"You will encounter nine additional Fontenot siblings, wives, children, uncles, aunts, cousins, his parents, and the matriarch's grandmother." You will have an advantage because you understand and speak French. The majority of his siblings are good, but be prepared for his mother, Marie, and his oldest sister, Janet, who behave similarly to her. I sensed something in my spirit telling me that Marie would not approve of me.

She might not be particularly welcoming, but the ancestors had instructed me to carry blessed oil to ward off evil spirits. Marie exudes arrogance and is deeply rooted in Creole culture. She loves Philip's ex, Suzanne. Just bring plenty of comfortable clothes—a dress or pantsuit—for mass on Sunday. Plus, you will need some mosquito repellant in a travel bottle that you can carry in your purse because you will need it as soon as you step off the plane.

In Houston, the mosquitoes are terrible; don't forget to pack your cowboy boots! I asked her if we were planning to go out and party, to which she replied, "Girl, yes, that's why I told you to bring your boots." Who's going to keep your baby? Aunt Faye Jessica says, "You will love her; she's nothing like her stuck-up sister." See you Sunday and be safe.

Our flight landed in Houston about thirty minutes before the Tidewater crew did. We got our luggage and waited for the others to arrive because we all had rented separate cars and were going to follow each other to Lake Charles. We all stayed at the same hotel due to the large number of guests arriving and the limited space in the family house. The men went to get the rental cars, turn on the air conditioner so they could cool off, and load some of the luggage. I helped Pricilla and Cheryl with the babies.

We stopped to eat before getting on the road. I fell asleep for thirty minutes because I could not sleep the night before. We finally made it to Lake Charles, checked into our hotel, and called the parents to let them know we had arrived. Among the hotel guests were a Dallas-based sibling and cousins.

When we finally arrived at his parents' house, many of his relatives were already present. I met other siblings, wives, husbands, aunts, uncles, and cousins. Many of the elderly family members only spoke French, which I had no problems with, and they seemed impressed. One of his aunts asked if I was Creole, and I explained that I was a language specialist, and French and Spanish were my concentrations. I had spent a summer in France and two summers in Haiti. I also explained that my ancestry included white, black, and

Native American people, but on the east coast, we were predominantly black and spoke English.

When it came time to meet his parents, a cold chill ran down my spine as we approached them. His father, Jacque, hugged me and welcomed me to the family, but his mother, Marie, was cold as ice with her cold gray eyes, and she only spoke in French, even though she could speak English. I surprised her by saying, "Bonsoir, Madame Fonte," in French, Marie responded, "Fine, thank you," in a detached manner, never looking directly at me.

I had only met one other person like her, and I learned from a very young age to keep my safe distance from her, that was my paternal grandmother. I continued to have a conversation with Jacque, but Marie got up and went over to speak to two other women.

Pricilla came over and said let's get something to eat. I overheard Marie say to the other women I don't like her, and she didn't even try to hide what she said. Not knowing who the other women were until Pricilla told me. It was Philip's ex-girlfriend Suzanne and his oldest sister Janet. Damn I knew this was going to be the longest two weeks.

Later that night, we made our way back to the hotel, and I was exhausted. We showered, crawled in the bed, and were out less than ten minutes. Normally, I would sleep with the television on, but that night, I was too tired.

This was my first Juneteenth celebration, and I wanted to enjoy everything. I went to the parade and shopped at vendors, but the most beautiful thing was hearing the church bells ring and knowing their meaning.

Later we journeyed out to his parents, where I met other family members, but the family member that I enjoyed the most was his grandmother or grand mere. She was beautiful, with long silver hair down to her waist and olive-colored skin that did not look a day over seventy. Good evening, grandmother. My name is Charlotte, and I am thrilled to meet you. I have heard many wonderful things about you. "Bonsoir Grand-mere. Jem'appelle Charlotte, and I'm very happy to meet you. J'ai entendu beaucoup de choses merrivilleuses sur vous." Grand-mere reaches for my hand and smiles.

Each day I would spend about thirty minutes with Grandma, telling her about my family, my job, and where I grew up. We went to listen to a Zydeco band the weekend of Juneteenth, and we had a good time. Many members of Philip's family were present, and we set up two large tables filled with nothing but family.

We went to New Orleans and Baton Rouge. We went horseback riding, showed me around Lake Charles, visited relatives, and before we knew it, it was time for us to return to Virginia. I went to speak to Grandmère before I left, letting her know how I learned so much from her—her history, recipes, life lessons, and that I loved her—and thanked her for welcoming me into her home. I only said goodbye to Marie; I avoided her as much as possible the whole two weeks. I thanked Jacque for welcoming me and how I enjoyed being in his home and his presence. We were all on the road by eight; our flight left at twelve fifty. The Tidewater crew flight left at one fifty. I reminded them about the Fourth Of July cookout with my parents. We hugged and kissed each other. "Will call when we get back tonight, said Jessica."

CHAPTER 10

....

The Drama Begins 2021

THE COUNTRY IS GRADUALLY OPENING UP. I THINK IT'S TOO soon; people are still dying. It's been three months since Lilian left for New York for her next movie. At the end of April, Lillian and Jacoby will be going to the Bahamas with a couple of directors, producers, and their wives for a two-week vacation.

I was overjoyed to see her when she informed me that she would undergo a ten-day quarantine before returning home, a practice common to all of them due to their familial responsibilities. They were staying at a private resort, they were traveling privately, they hired their own chef, and they had food delivered daily. Lois mailed her package overnight to ensure it arrived on time. I asked her about protection and birth control, which I talk to all my children about. She called to ask me to send her all of these outfits because she wasn't going out shopping. Lois and I went to her room, where we found the outfits she had texted me about. Later that night, I zoomed with her to ensure we had everything she needed, including her passport. During our Zoom conversation, I showed her everything she asked for, along with all the accessories, and she blew kisses thanking me. Lillian tells me, Mama, that we've discussed having a baby. No, I didn't want this for my baby, but she is twenty-seven years old. There was nothing I could say or do to make her change her mind. By the time I reached her age, I had only one child, unaware that there were five more in the wings. Once she got there, I asked her to facetime me and blew her kisses.

One night, Lillian initiates a FaceTime call, apologizing for not calling sooner, and proceeds to share her recent activities with me. She describes the villa they were staying in, along with its amenities. She had a beautiful tan, and I reminded her to please be careful in the sun. I asked about Jacoby, and she tells me that he and the other men were sitting by the pool drinking cognac and smoking Cuban cigars.

As she began to change the conversation, a look of concern came upon her face. Mama Shelly is down here with her family on vacation; somehow, she found out Jacoby is down here as well, and she has tried to speak to him by calling the villa, and she even showed up here twice, but the guards would not allow her on the grounds. He has been very forthcoming, and he has told the staff not to put her calls through. She can't contact him by cell because he has blocked her whole family.

Lillian says, "I told him he needed to speak to her, clear the air, and wish her well, but let her know that their relationship is over." He said that she cries and throws tantrums when she doesn't get her way, and I don't deal with drama from grown women. I asked her if she needed me to send her siblings down for some moral support, and she said no, she had it; they only had a couple of days left before they left to come back.

Despite testing negative before leaving, they remained in Atlanta quarantine. After that, they would stay at our house for a few days before he returned to California. The next morning, I received a strange text from Lois, which prompted me to pull up the article and video. There was a confrontation at the airport where Shelly approaches Jacoby and tells him, "His career is over, and he can't make it in the industry without her father's money. He will never finance any of his projects." He keeps moving forward, refusing to succumb to her self-centered displays. She grabs his arm, glances at Lillian, and declares, "You are temporary, and he will come back to me because he loves me. When he gets sick of you, he will dump your ass in the trash where you belong, bitch."

Jacoby quickly pulls away from her and proceeds towards customs. The customs agents observe the commotion, call them into an office, check their passports, and allow them to leave, all while Shelly continues to scream insults. The video is available on social media and tabloid television shows. I texted Lillian and asked if she was alright, because I was pissed. Before I had a chance to call her, Jacoby and Lillian Facetimed me. Jacoby's first words were, "Mrs. Fontenot, I am so sorry that you had to see that." I am not a drama person, and Shelly believes she can throw tantrums and make a scene in order for me to stay with her. I don't need her dad's money to further my career. Matter of fact, he wanted to finance a couple of my projects, and I said no. My business partners advised me not to allow him in because he has some unscrupulous business associates, and I have worked diligently to secure my business. I don't need her father, his money, or his business for the success of my company."

I told him I was concerned for my daughter's safety, and she said, Mama, I am ok; please don't worry. We will see you in a week. "Jacoby, take care of my baby." He replied, "I will. I'll protect her life as if it were mine. That night at dinner, everyone was extremely quiet, and there was tension in the air. I was certain that everyone had witnessed it, and just like me, they were in a state of shock. Raymond asked, "Have you spoken to Lillian?" Yes, this morning I replied." Bella replied, "I have left numerous messages, and she has not called back." "That's her way of telling you to mind your business," I replied. "Mama, she's our sister; are you aware of the numerous texts and phone calls I've received regarding the content on these gossip sites?" "Yes, what do you suppose I've been doing today?" I only spoke to certain family members, just as I am speaking to you now. I spoke to Jacoby mostly, but she was there too. Lillian is fine." Before coming to Atlanta, they want to make sure that they are okay. Although their tests came back negative, they want to confirm their condition before continuing their journey. She will be here in a week. Jacoby just doesn't know what he is in for next week.

CHAPTER 11

·····························

The Return 2021

I WAS IN THE GARDEN WHEN SHE ENTERED THE HOUSE, hollering at the top of her lungs, "Mama," and before I could get up, she was all over me. She had been absent for nearly five months. She had never been absent for such an extended period. I held her for a while before telling her to let me take a closer look. She had picked up a little weight, but it looked good on her. Being out in the sun made her hair have blondish highlights, and it fit well with her dark tan. They bring all these bags in, and I asked her, Did you go shopping while in the Bahamas? Of course she replied.

I looked back, seeing Jacoby standing like a scared child, and I reached my hands out to him. I promise not to hurt you; please come and give me a hug, to which he responded with a long, heartfelt smile.

Everyone knew dinner is always served at six thirty, slowly everyone comes in and is seated by six thirty. My brother had not been to dinner in over a month came to dinner tonight, and Gerald blessed the food.

I had to break the tension at the table because I was afraid there was going to be a major explosion at my dinner table. "Jacoby, despite their adulthood, my children maintain an extremely close bond. My boys are very protective of my girls, and vice versa. I am giving you the opportunity to explain the situation to my family before anyone becomes upset."

Jacoby began to speak. "I want you all to understand that Lilian is not a rebound. When we started working together last year, my previous relationship was a wash. Lillian and I became friends, and that's what relationships should be based on: friendship. I learned about her, including her likes, dislikes, family, parents, growing up, and schools. Lillian discovered the same thing about me. My family resides on the west coast. I grew up in Detroit; our upbringings were different. I continue to learn about her, just as she does about me. I regret that Lillian found herself entangled in a situation beyond her control. Shelly is a spoiled woman who throws tantrums when she doesn't get her way and believes her father is the solution to all her problems. She believes her father possesses the power to either control or destroy the lives of others. I have no business dealings with her father. I founded my production company with legitimate business partners. Although her father has a reputation for engaging in dubious business dealings, he is a decent man with whom I have had some pleasant conversations. Nevertheless, he does not control my life, just as she does not. I am deeply in love with Lillian, and I am committed to protecting her life at all costs." Frederick asked him, "What made you so attractive to my sister?" "Her eyes are the path to her soul. "I damn near choked. Many years ago, I heard the same words from Philip. Hearing him say those words was like watching myself through the window. I just hope it does not turn out like my marriage."

CHAPTER 12

Decision 1980

MY ROOMMATE AND I DECIDED NOT TO RENEW OUR APARTMENT lease. I asked Philip if we could become roommates, and he was fine with it. I didn't understand why you were paying half on an apartment when you were never there. I moved in, and our relationship intensified.

Philip asked, "Have you ever thought of getting married?" "Yes, to the right person, who understands that it's not a seasonal relationship; it's forever. I don't believe in divorce. I asked, "Is it because your brothers are married and have families?" "No, I want someone to love and love me in return," replied Philip.

"Didn't you have that with Suzanne?" "No, all she wanted was a creole and a man she could control with her father's money, and I am not that man, he said." I noticed how she would watch Mama, and she would say things that complimented my mother's harshness with my dad, and I knew then that she wasn't the right woman for me." "Your mother dislikes me," I told him. "I understand that it's due to your unpredictable nature, but don't worry; she doesn't like many of my married sibling's spouses." That's why she is always bypassed, and we take them to Gran-mere. Gran-mere didn't want our father to marry our mother; however, when she became pregnant, Daddy, being the man he is, decided to marry her. "Well, are you considering marriage?" You haven't figure it out by now and just laugh."

I needed to make some decisions quickly, especially after he informed me that he had received orders for Norfolk, Virginia. There was a Nancy Wilson concert. That weekend, Philip's siblings and their spouses came up to hang out, as did my siblings and their spouses. After the concert, we all headed to a jazz club for drinks and dinner. Philip expressed his desire to make this occasion truly memorable. You are the love of my life. When I first met you, I knew you were the one, and I didn't even know your name. I love you, Charlotte; will you be my wife?" "Yes," I replied without any hesitation.

CHAPTER 13

·····························

It's Official 2021

SHELLY AND JACOBY ARE NO LONGER A COUPLE. IT'S ALL ON THE tabloids, talk shows, and social media. Shelly is talking very badly about him; even her parents are saying nasty things about him. Whenever someone questions Jacoby, he consistently responds with silence. No one is speaking about Lillian; one day, when I returned home, a media crew was outside my gate, attempting to obtain answers, but we managed to drive past them. Good thing we have tinted windows on my truck. As soon as I stepped inside, the tabloids were abuzz with stories about Shelly's and Jacoby's breakup on the television. Jacoby was dating Shelly and the women in the video at the same time. Jacoby was not taking any chances with Lillian's safety, so he hired security for Lillian when she traveled or left the estate.

I asked if she was home, and she was sitting in the kitchen. I just hugged her really tight and asked if she was okay. Mama I am fine. Jacoby has sold his LA home and is closing on his ATL home. I asked her about her next job, and she is now in ATL for her next movie. In a month, I will undergo COVID precautions and participate in the same movie as Jacoby. I asked, "So when will you be leaving this time?" I'll be here for a week, then off to ATL for the next six weeks. I want to make sure you are okay. I am Mama, but I have something to tell you: I'm pregnant.

I knew, but I was waiting for you to tell me. I know Mama and Jacoby is excited. This will be the first grandchild for his parents. No one but you and his parents knows. Have you seen a doctor yet? Got an appointment tomorrow morning. Will you go with me? Yes, I replied. Do you have any morning sicknesses? I mixed my herbal tea and drank it at night. I asked, "What about throwing up?" Once I started drinking the herbal tea, all symptoms disappeared. I just want to get through this movie. We should finish it in six weeks. I just hope I'm not showing. The doctor's appointment went well; he gave her a doctor to see in Atlanta, and he will call the doctor personally to set up special appointments.

CHAPTER 14

. . . .

Twenty Years 2001

I CAN'T BELIEVE PHILIP AND I HAVE BEEN MARRIED FOR TWENTY years, and we have six children. Philip did not want a long engagement, so time was of the essence. Seven months after his proposal to me, we tied the knot. We moved to Hampton, Va., because I did not want to live on the other side of the water. I hated to leave my job in Northern Virginia, but I did get a position in the area that was similar to the one I left. Moving, preparing for a wedding, and trying to get another job were exhausting. Because I never took time off, I had a lot of free days. I ended my school year just before Memorial Day weekend to get the house settled.

We came from different religious backgrounds, so we found a church and a minister willing to marry us. My girlfriend, a fashion designer, created my gown for me. I showed her a photo of my mama's prom gown, and after many fittings, it was just the right amount of tulle material. I had a designer wedding gown, and it was beautiful. My number was seven, so there were seven groomsmen and bridesmaids. Marie chose not to attend, citing the need for someone to stay with Grand mere and allow Aunt Faye to take on his mother's role.

- Our wedding and reception were beautiful; everything ran as it was supposed to. We went to the Bahamas for our honeymoon, then to Lake Charles to spend some time with Grand Mere before returning home. After we were married for three months, I discovered I was pregnant, and from that point on, I had another baby every two years, with the exception of Shauna and the twins. Marie told me that Shauna's developmental problems must have come from your side of the family, as we don't typically produce mentally retarded babies. I hung up on her and told Philip that I would never speak to her again.

Philip decided to remain in the military for four more years. With a war going on, he would not be involved with the war directly. He was a program developer; he would observe how troops were being trained with the programs that he developed.

When Raymond and Shauna were born, he was very attentive to them and me, but when the twins arrived, I noticed a change in his behavior. He began to never show interest. After the twins' birth, I requested a vasectomy from him, but he refused and refused to sign for the tying of my tubes, leading to a heated argument. What I began to notice was the way he treated me—never a compliment, no flowers, no rubbing of the feet, no special dinners, no nothing. One night I asked him was he still in love with me, and he said yes without looking at me.

What was really noticeable was when we returned from Lake Charles, or when he spoke to Marie; it was like he was under a spell. It was about a week later before he would return to our bed. He would sleep in his office on the pull-out bed. When he returned, he could not get enough of me, and during our lovemaking, he would constantly apologize and tell me how much he loved me, which was very confusing to me.

I was the one who met with all their teachers and attended all their activities and sporting events, and it was a lot. They all spoke French and Spanish, plus they knew sign language. I read bedtime stories, set out their clothes until they began to pick out their own, checked homework, and worked with them on special projects until the older kids helped out some. Everything fell on me, when Raymond went to college, my parents went to the local games for Ernest, and Bella and I took Shauna and Lillian sometimes with me to Raymond's games. If it was on the weekend, we all went.

I taught them about money and opened up accounts for each of them. They turned sixteen, they received ATM cards, and they had to manage their money, and their accounts were not allowed to drop below a certain amount.

I taught them how to drive. They couldn't drive at night or transport anyone other than their siblings in the car. Upon purchasing their own car, they were responsible for covering their own insurance costs, and a ticket would result in a three-month suspension from driving. I planned summer vacations for us, and not once did Philip attend. I talked to him about it; all he said was that his job kept him busy. As the children grew older, they began to help out with Shauna, Gerald, and Lillian, and they noticed their father's lack of interest.

When Ernest was about fifteen years old on a Friday night, he asked his father why the entire family had to travel to Lake Charles for Juneteenth. Our grandmother Marie does not acknowledge us. She refers to us as "the bastards" from Virginia. You barely acknowledge us when you are here, but you want to parade us around like puppets and act like an attentive father, which you are not.

Before I knew it, he backhanded Ernest, and Raymond tackled him and punched him in the face. He told them both to get the hell out. I stepped in and said, "Hell no, you will not be putting my kids out. This is nothing new; I have been talking to you about it for years. You have never participated in any of their activities, attended any sporting events, or done anything else. When you get around your family, you want to act like you are the father of the year." Philip replied, "If they don't leave, I will." "Bye," I said; there's nothing standing between you and the door but air, and don't expect us to go down to Lake Charles."

He packed a bag and left. I called Pricilla after I got everyone settled and told her what had happened. He had already called, but his story was totally different. Pricilla and I had conversations about these issues many times, but at least her husband helped some, but the majority of the tasks in my house still fell on me.

Something was not right. The old souls repeatedly communicated to me that significant changes are imminent in your household. I have been so busy trying to keep my family in sync. So many things have slipped by without my attention. It's possible that this arrangement was intentional. Tonight I will start to investigate. I began my investigation by scrutinizing credit cards, cell phone bills, and bank statements to identify any discrepancies, and I found that everything was aligning perfectly.

CHAPTER 15

· ·

They Knew

AFTER PHILIP LEFT THAT NIGHT, I INSTRUCTED EVERYONE TO STAY inside, try to get some sleep, and in the morning, we would go to our favorite breakfast spot, have a good breakfast, and then return home so we could hold a family meeting later.

Once we returned home, I asked, "Ernest, what made you speak to your father the way you did?" "Mama, I am tired of watching you bust your butt to maintain this house and ensure our well-being." Without Lois, Mama Liza, and Papa J, you would be exhausted from juggling everything, including work. What does Philip do? "Nothing but a sperm provider if you ask me," Bella replied. "What's wrong with him?" asked Gerald. He barely speaks. No interaction with us at all. When he's here, he doesn't even come to eat dinner or engage in conversation with us. "What's wrong with us?" Lillian asked. "Nothing!" I replied.

Raymond instructs Lillian to take Shauna into the kitchen, and they can have some cookies. When they were away, he said, Mama, "there is something you need to know." Remember when Sam and I took his mother to the airport in

Norfolk? When we went inside the airport, I saw him kissing Suzanne. He was so engrossed in her that he didn't see me." "Did you all know?" They all answered yes. "I am sorry," Bella asked. "Why are you apologizing? You did nothing."

After meeting with the children, Lois and I sat in the backyard on the patio and drank a glass of wine. The next thing I knew, Pricilla walked out on the patio looking for us. I told Bella to get her aunt a wineglass, and she poured herself a little. The kids look beat. I don't believe anyone slept in this house except for Shauna, as she doesn't understand the gravity of what happened last night. I asked, "Are you packed and ready for Juneteenth in Lake Charles?" Pricilla replied, "My two youngest have bad colds, and I decided not to take them down in all that humid weather, so the kids and I are staying here. Donnell was fine with it. What would I do if you weren't there with me? Your husband and Donnell are leaving on Wednesday." "Thank you for informing me," I responded. Whenever I call him, his secretary consistently responds with an excuse that he's not in. I'm pretty sure he told her that if I call, he's not available, but I got a rude awakening from him.

I went to his office on Monday, and when his secretary began to speak, I walked past her and politely closed the door. "This is not a negotiation; meet me at the Crab House in Hampton at five, or I will personally deliver everything in this notebook to your commanding officer tomorrow morning." Margret, his wife, is a close friend of mine. Therefore, refrain from engaging in playful behavior with me. I watched the color drain from his face as I got up and walked out. The book contained nothing, but he was unaware of it.

CHAPTER 16

· ·

No Excuses

I GOT TO THE CRAB HOUSE AT FOUR THIRTY BECAUSE I WANTED those spicy crab balls and a salad. I would be taking food home with me because my kids love the food here as well. When Philip arrived, he came over to the table that was isolated from others; that's the way I wanted, plus it's a Monday; there would not be that many people there tonight. The waiter came over and asked him what he was drinking. "Hennessy, on the rocks," and she gave him a menu. "You not drinking, he asked?" "No, because I want to make sure I hear you correctly."

"Why?" I asked. You had an opportunity to be with Suzanne in the beginning. I didn't chase behind you. You asked me to marry you. After Shauna or the twins were born, you would not have a vasectomy. Philip responded, "That didn't stop you from getting your tubes tied after Lillian was born, did it?" "No, I responded. "I had a challenging pregnancy with Lillian, and you knew it. You didn't attend the births of any of our children, and without the support of Pricilla, Lois, Big Ma, and my mom, I might not have survived." However, I now understand that he didn't care. He does nothing to help out with the children. He never helps them with school, activities, or anything else. "What have the children done to you?" I asked. "You didn't correct Marie when she called them "the bastards from Virginia." "Mama never said that," Philip replied. I looked at him with disbelief. "Ask your children! Ask Aunt Faye or your other family members.

"You still have not answered my question: Why did you decide to have an affair with Suzanne? I have all the information, including phone calls, texts, vacations, and photos. "We have a daughter together," he replied. I burst out laughing. They had conducted a DNA test; this child was not his. I burst out laughing. See, he thinks I am some little mousy woman that doesn't know people.

Philip asked, "What about that land you own?" "I don't have any land; that's Daddy's land, and I am to handle it in case something happens to him, and Mama is not capable of handling it." Why didn't you tell me you were a root woman? I nearly choked on my drink, laughing at his antics. "If I were a root woman, you wouldn't be with Suzanne or still be alive."

Philip informed me he filed for divorce and asked for half of the land. "Go for it." I replied, "By the way, your son saw you kissing that bitch Suzanne in the airport. When will you be moving from the house? Philip informed me that he didn't intend to move out and would be sleeping in his office. I informed him he needed to get his things out as soon as possible when no one is home. The home we once shared will be mine, at least until Lillian turns eighteen. Philip complained that he could not afford paying for two places, and I had no sympathy for him.

Philip informed me I was being vindictive because he didn't love me anymore. He said it took him a long time to realize that I was a rebound relationship. Suzanne was the only woman he had ever loved, and he would spend the rest of his life with her.

"What about your children, I asked?" "They all are adults, except Gerald and Lillian, and you can finish raising them." What he said knocked the wind out of me, but I refused to allow him to see how hurt I was. I had ordered my takeout earlier and asked if it was ready. When the waitress brought it to me, I informed her that Philip would take care of the bill. "Good luck Philip but remember everything glitters aint gold." When I got to the car, I left the restaurant parking lot only to go to a Hardees parking lot. The tears flowed like the Jordan River.

The ancestors came that night, and I cried myself to sleep. "We warned you, just like the others. You are not the first, and you will not be the last."

CHAPTER 17

The thrill is gone, but the fight is on!

THIS FOOL HAS LOST HIS DAMN MIND. HE IS UNAWARE THAT HE is still on active duty, and he is daring me to present the evidence of his adulterous affair with Suzanne to his commander. He is in the process of divorcing me due to allegations of unorthodox religious practices. When I went to see my lawyer, Jennifer Sawyer, she reviewed the papers I had received and suggested that we should proceed to arbitration to try to resolve this issue. She pointed out that he has no proof of any of this, but you have access to the information. If he is aware, as I am, he would seek a divorce, grant you what you desire, and then let the matter rest if he wishes to maintain his benefits.

Our first meeting was one week away. My lawyer prepared a copy of the evidence I had, included a video recording of our son recounting his experiences at Norfolk Airport, and provided proof of a ticket for Suzanne that Philip had paid for. In our first meeting, he told me how I grew herbs in the windowsill and how I would use them to treat minor illnesses and injuries. Philip described a practice I used to keep evil out of the house: certain times of the month I would not have sex, and that I had a safe that only I had the combination to with how to put spells on people. There was a video where Marie described me as evil, claiming that she knew people like me who weren't Christians.

After listening to this garbage for about an hour, I had time to explain my actions. I explained that his mother had never liked me and had referred to our children as the "bastards from Virginia." I used processed store-bought herbs but preferred the taste of fresh herbs. We all had minor illnesses and scratches, so I used them. My lawyer inquired about Philip's relationship with Suzanne. He stated that they were friends. At that point, my lawyer presented him with a variety of documents, including cell phone and credit card records dating back up to five years, as well as video clips featuring them in various locations such as the Bahamas, Mexico, Houston, Hawaii, and a video of our oldest son Raymond recounting his experiences at the airport. He remained silent as my lawyer inquired about the potential consequences if his commanding officer received this information. He said nothing. We ended the meeting and decided to meet again to figure out how to handle finances.

You listening to people who never had your best interest in mind." If you had considered your own best interests, you would have corrected your mother when she initially referred to our children as "bastards." After realizing the damaging nature of the information I had, he decided to continue making house payments until

Lillian turned eighteen. This required a monthly payment of twelve hundred dollars, which would cover the child support of Lillian, Gerald, Bella, and Ernest. Because of her handicap, Shauna would receive military health insurance and a military identification card for the rest of her life. When he retired, I would receive half of his retirement and maintain my military identification and medical benefits for life, unless I remarried. Philip agreed to my demands for a divorce and changed his plea to an uncontested one. He retired before the divorce was final. In 2006. I received a package. Inside was a plaque and certificate for being a wife to an active-duty marine for twenty five years. DAMN!

I called him, and he said, "Why are you calling me? We are divorced, and we have nothing to say to each other." I replied, "I need paperwork to get the military identification for Shauna, Lillian, Gerald, and myself." You can continue to use your current military identification. I said over the phone, "We can't; you are no longer on active duty." You have five days to deliver the documents to me before I hang up. My heart sank deeply; tears streamed down my face. What had I done to deserve this treatment?

CHAPTER 18

Hurt, pain, sorrow, history…..
But there is healing!

ALTHOUGH I FINALIZED MY DIVORCE SIX MONTHS AGO, THE pain I felt remained as fresh as the day I discovered Philip was having an affair. I portrayed myself as a strong Black woman; I always kept a level head regardless of the situation at home and at work. My children were protecting me from their father's affair; had I shown some act of weakness, I questioned myself. I recognized the need for counseling as I experienced a profound sense of internal turmoil. My lupus flareups were one on top of another, and each time my steroid doses were higher.

One night there was a terrible thunderstorm, and Shauna, terrified, came and crawled in my bed. She realized I was crying and patted me on the back, saying, "I love you, Mommie." The next day Shauna asks Gerald to take her to Big Ma's house, and she tells her, "Mama cried all night." I kept telling her I loved her. Big Ma is the matriarch of the family; she is the oldest. On the phone, she calls those who accept their gift and tells them that it's time to return home, as someone is in distress. Slaves arrived in America with everything stripped from them. They lost everything they brought with them, including their religion, language, and names. Slave owners viewed everything as witchery, evil, and voodoo, forcing Sarah to practice her gift in secrecy. This was due to the white man's lack of understanding of African traditions and his attempts to suppress them. Many succumbed to the master, but many didn't.

Big Ma knew I was hurting, but she knew how private I was, and she was waiting for the time to call others. When Shauna told her about me crying at night, she knew it was that time. Everyone knew what they had to bring. This time Big Ma called her sister, my mother, and said, "I know you don't practice the old ways, but your daughter needs you." Eliza said, "I know." Everyone will be there Sunday morning at the old homestead by the creek at the crack of dawn. You can ride with me, Tilda; that's my big ma's name.

I was surprised when I got there to see so many cars. There was a barbecue going on, and food was everywhere. The men were doing all the cooking, and we had a large screen in the dining area where we could eat in peace with no flies. A long table held the food, resembling a buffet. My uncle blessed the food, and we all got in line. There was plenty of food, and everyone ate a good southern dinner. I looked up and saw my boys pulling up, which shocked me. Gerald said we were not about to miss out on this cookout. Out-of-town guests lodged at a nearby hotel approximately five miles from our ancestral home, which my great-great grandparents Moses and Elizabeth Bercier Bryan inherited in 1875. Elizabeth was Sarah's great, great granddaughter.

Over the years, many changes occurred, and one of my cousins lived on the property.

We all left about eight to go to the hotel and I was beat so after my shower I went to sleep, because tomorrow was an early start.

Someone knocked on my door around five fifteen that morning, making sure everyone was up. I woke up Shauna, Lillian, and Bella and told them to get up so we could get ready to go. My boys were in the next room, but I allowed them to continue to sleep.

Around six thirty, we arrived at the family homestead, surrounded by numerous cars. All we could see were women dressed in white, adorned with purple belts, our heads bound in white, all of us heading towards the water. The color purple reminded us of Sarah's palms. When Sarah arrived in South Carolina, she was a slave on a plantation that produced indigo, which left a permanent stain on the palms of her hands. At the age of forty, a small farmer named Harry Bercier of Edgecombe County, N.C., purchased Sarah, her husband Lewis, and all eight of her children. Sarah assumed the role of family cook, while her family worked as field hands and seamstresses. Lewis, on the other hand, worked as Bercier driver until emancipation.

Harry Bercier didn't believe in breaking up families; he felt keeping households together got better work out of the slaves. Bercier never had any runaway slaves or troublemakers on his farm. During her enslavement, Bercier permitted Sarah's children to marry slaves on other farms and plantations. A slave who had traveled with Sarah from Africa gave her a brick of indigo on the night they were preparing for their journey to North Carolina, reminding her that this was the first stop of their journey in this land. It is important to pass down everything from our homeland to your children and their children's children. That's where dancing and praying came from.

Once at the creek, someone came up beside me and grabbed my hand; it was my sister Carol. My eyes filled with tears. Someone helped Big Ma into the creek, and she started speaking. "We are all descended from a slave woman from Africa named Sarah, who ignored her gift. Her attraction and love for a man lured her away from her village, leading to her capture." We all failed by not following our intuitions or our ancestors and suffered the consequences, but we all ultimately succeeded." Some of us took longer than others, but we made it. Big Ma gave me the nickname "Baby Girl." I've been witnessing her internal suffering for far too long. The pain you have endured has penetrated your heart and soul, and you need our help to restore you from the guilt and shame you feel. She reached out to me and said, "Come to me."

I walked out to the creek, and others made a circle where Big Ma was. Tears were streaming down my face. My mama Eliza, my girls Bella, Lillian, and Shana, and my sister Carol made a circle around me and held hands. My other relatives made a circle around them, until there were four separate circles. You could tell that we were Sarah's daughters. The matriarchs of their family, who recognized their gift at a young age, bestowed an indigo stain on the top part of their middle finger. Big Ma touched the water, dipped her finger into the indigo, and gently touched the middle of my forehead, leaving a tiny stain that would remain for a lifetime. The circle merged into a larger one, and they began to pray, dance, and chant, accompanied by the rhythmic movement of a stick and tambourine, as tears streamed down my face. Big Ma continues to speak. "Take away the guilt, dear Lord. She did nothing wrong; she was a good wife and a good mother, but like many of us she met, she married a man who did her wrong. Big Ma said, Take away the hurt and pain that lingers in her heart and soul; bring her back from the darkness; let the light shine in her heart and soul again."

I began to feel the spirit of my ancestors, and I began to chant. My body began to move to the beat of the stick and the tambourine. "My sisters continue to teach these young'uns the right way to use their gift; teach them about our ancestors and where their gift came from, for if it were not for the ancestors, we would not be where we are today. Then Big Ma prayed, "To continue to bless this family and the generations to come," to which we all responded, "Ase." Mama embraced me in a way she had never done before. My sister, my girls, and I shared a group hug. Big Ma said, "Something significant is on its way." Use it to teach others. Help those who are less fortunate. "I helped her as we moved to our cars and hugged her like my life depended on it. On my way back to the hotel, I was listening to "It's over now" by Bishop Marvin Winan's, and it had a whole new meaning for me.

CHAPTER 19

· ·

Friends

IT WAS THE END OF A SCHOOL YEAR. RAYMOND GRADUATED from college and decided to return home. In addition to his desire to assist, Raymond had secured positions as a teacher and a head basketball coach. I attempted to persuade Raymond to move into his own apartment, but he expressed a preference for staying at home to provide a stable environment for his younger brothers. At their age, they needed it; furthermore, he did not trust Philip, and that gave us time to put away money.

This time, two of my children were heading off to college. In two years Shauna, Frederick, and Bella would be graduating together; that only left Gerald and Lillian. Lois continued to work for me. Lois was more than an employee; she was family. Aunt Faye called and begged us to come down for Juneteenth. I told her that I would check with the kids, and I would get back with her. All the kids decided they did not want to go. They didn't want to see their father, which was the main reason. That night, I called Pricilla and informed her about the phone call from Aunt Faye. Pricilla explained that her family would not be attending this year due to Donnell's inability to take the week off, and they had decided to travel in July to spend time with their family. That sounded better, and I would ask the kids if that would be a suitable time to go. I would love to see Jacque and Aunt Faye; furthermore, I am stronger now.

I suggested to Pricilla that we could celebrate Juneteenth here. We could create space; they could spend the night here with the kids; and we could cook and prepare gumbo together. Donnell said he would order some Louisiana crawfish and just have a wonderful time. Pricilla stated, "Philip has spoken to Donnell numerous times since he moved to Houston." They talked about his new position and how he liked it out there, but Philip never asked about his children. One night, while Donnell was on the speaker phone, I overheard him questioning how and why he could leave his children behind without even asking about them. I heard Philip say they were never my children; they were Charlotte's children. Donnell responded, "That's because you were never there for them, and you lived in the same house." Donnell may have spoken to him once since that conversation."

That night, I spoke to the children, informing them that their Uncle Donnell and his family would not be going to Lake Charles for Juneteenth, and they would be going a month later. Would they like to go and spend some time with Aunt Faye and Papa Jacque? Not all of the family would be present. Only the locals, aware that their father wouldn't be present, the children expressed their excitement. I called Pricilla and told her we would be going as well, and I would make our reservations as soon as I got off the phone. Are you going to stay in the same hotel? I said yes, along with making reservations for an SUV.

The next morning, I went out to the beach, sitting in the swing as I usually do when the mornings were not too hot. A gentleman walked up and said, My friend, where have you been hiding? Joseph was there. Together, the two of us served on a couple of school committees, and our children were around the same age and participated on some of the same athletic teams. Joe's wife passed away a few years ago, leaving him with the responsibility of raising five children. His sister had relocated from the north to assist him, as she had recently retired. You know, I had heard that you were going through a divorce." "Yes, we finalized the divorce six months ago," I replied. "How are you?" Joe asked. "Much better," I replied. "I'm glad to hear that, but to be honest, I wouldn't recognize the man if he walked up, as he never attended any of the children's activities." Since he was in the Marines, I assumed he was part of the special forces or something similar, given his lack of presence. He was an officer, as I explained. He never left the area unless it was necessary for TDY, and he never made time for the children. I found out he was having an affair with his high school sweetheart. It was painful for a while, but I have since come to the realization that it is preferable to allow a man to depart rather than continue to make you look like a fool. Joe said, "You are right about that."

"Have you started dating anyone?" "No interest," I replied. "I have four children at home under eighteen, and they take up a lot of my time. Furthermore, my parents, along with my big mama, are aging. My plate is full." "What about some adult time? Joe asked. Having dinner with friends your age. You need that." "I do get together with my sister-in-law every blue moon; we meet up, go shopping, and do lunch or dinner." "You should schedule grown-up time at least twice a month; you'll be surprised at how much it improves your mood." When my wife passed away, I became deeply involved with the children. I was masking my grief by not really acknowledging it. I finally broke down one night at home when I thought I was on top of everything. I got a call from the school nurse at home telling me my sixteen-year-old daughter was pregnant. I thank God my sister had moved in. I cried my heart out trying to figure out what I was doing wrong. I ended up going to counseling. For myself and all my children, I went to family counseling. My children were mourning. I told them if they needed to talk about the death of their mother, I was there, but they didn't. Their grades began to decline; they began to act out in school, neglected their chores, and not assisting their younger siblings. I replied that my children were not used to their dad being around. Only Lois, the housekeeper, and I were familiar with their surroundings. Thank you for the information, and I'll keep an eye out for any signs.

"How about some adult time? I am not seeking a relationship, I replied. Joe said, "Don't take it personal; if things were different, I would love to have a relationship with you." I looked at that as a compliment, but I am not interested in a relationship. Being divorced is still new to me. I explained to him we are having a Juneteenth celebration and would love for him and his family to join us. My family and in-laws will be present, and we've opened the pool. We would have plenty of food. The kids know each other, and everyone should have a wonderful time.

As our conversation continued over time, Joe and I began to encourage each other to do things outside the norm. So one night he called me and said, "I know you have a swimsuit, so put it on, and I'm going to pick you up around nine in the morning." We are heading to Damn Neck, where you will be swimming in the ocean. I reminded him that I don't do ocean water, and he said I know. You will step outside of your box, and I will join you. The temperature should be eighty-three, which is perfect for our two-hour stay. Remember how you got me to eat raw oysters, and they still taste nasty? Is this a payback I requested? No, I just want you to get over your fear. OK, I'll be ready. The following morning, we set out for Damn Neck, where the majority of the daily traffic had vanished. Once we arrived, we set up our umbrella and made our way to the water. At first, I was frightened by the force and height of the waves. Additionally, when the tide receded, the sand beneath my feet dug a hole. However, he reassured me by holding my hands, and I relished the experience. We ended up spending over half of the day together. The water hit me, the sun tanned me, even applied the strongest sunblock available. When I returned home I took a shower, checked on where my children were, and took a long nap. Bella would not allow the others to wake me up; she told them, "Mama needs the rest. How often does she sleep during the middle of the day?"

Before I knew it, Juneteenth was here. I had prepared by getting food; Pricilla came over the day before, and we prepped food, made gumbo, had fun talking smack, and drank more wine than we should have, and I told her about my friendship with Joe. Pricilla gave me a look. No, my sister, I explained, "We both lost spouses; we have children around the same age; we both have help inside the house; we are just friends." Neither one of us wants a relationship. His wife passed away a few years ago, and I also lost mine to the ozone layer, so we support each other by offering advice. We are pushing each other to think creatively, which brings us joy. He encouraged me to prioritize self-care by scheduling adult time; he took me to Damn Neck and took me into the ocean, where I thoroughly enjoyed myself. "So that's why you got such a pretty tan," Pricilla replied. I laughed and said, "You will meet him tomorrow; our kids go to school together and play sports together; they have been going to school together since kindergarten. We knew each other prior because we served on committees together; I knew his late wife prior to her death." The following day, everyone arrived at noon. I had prepared most of the food, the kids were playing in the pool, Big Ma, Mama, and Daddy were inside the screen porch, and I had set up a screen tent to ensure everyone could eat in peace, free from flies, while music played. Donnell arrived with Pricilla's three boys, and the girls had joined her the day before. We explained to everyone the purpose of our Juneteenth celebration, then proceeded to eat. The rest of the day was filled with joy and excitement. Joe's family blended right in with my in-laws and family; it was a big success. The kids wore themselves out in the pool. I put Donnell and Pricilla in my guest room because Raymond had turned his father's study into his bedroom. Joe departed around nine, while Mama, Daddy, and Big Mama left before the sun set. After we finished putting away the food, cleaned the kitchen, checked the outside conditions, and washed all the towels, Lois crawled onto the couch and fell asleep, and I crashed, grateful for a successful day.

CHAPTER 20

I can't believe this is happening!

EVERY WEDNESDAY, LIKE CLOCKWORK, I TAKE BIG MA TO Farmers Market for fresh vegetables. She's getting older, and I noticed she had slowed down quite a bit. I'd take her to the market for fresh vegetables, and then we'd go to this little country market for fresh meat if she needed it. That gave us a lot of one-on-one time. I saw her at least every day, to make sure that there was nothing that she went without. Some evenings, Joe and I would go get her and take her to the beach, and he would push her in the wheelchair down the boardwalk because she loved the water.

On the way home this particular Wednesday, she asked me to stop at the corner store and get her a bag of pork skins. While I was there, I noticed that the lottery had reached a jackpot of one point seven billion. I thought, "What the heck, it's not like I'm going to win any money," so I asked the machine to select seven tickets for me, as if I had some extra cash to spare. If you don't play, you don't stand a chance to win, I thought. I placed the tickets in my wallet, headed back to the car, and handed her the bag of skins. Sunday morning I was preparing for church, and the news stated one person won the whole lottery, but it did not say where. I figured it was someone in California or New York, because those two states are the ones that win the most, especially when there is a big payoff. No one in Virginia never wins. I went to church; Lois cooked dinner on Friday, so I picked up some small items and went home to warm up the meal. After dinner, I was watching the evening news. The news anchors discussed the unique ticket, including all of the numbers available at the store where I bought it. They even showed the store. I grabbed my purse, checked my tickets, and found all the numbers on the last one. I signed my name and locked it in my safe. I was not taking any chances.

I called my closest friend and asked her if I had paid for her round-trip ticket from Raleigh, and could she come to Virginia? Lacey started questioning me about the situation, and I assured her that I would discuss it with her tomorrow. However, I needed her to find the best accountant she knew in this area, as it was her line of work. I told her I would call her back tonight, and she could print out her ticket. I did just that. Her flight left at eight in the morning, and she would be in Norfolk by nine thirty. I contacted her again after fifteen minutes, providing her with the necessary details to print her ticket. I asked Raymond to pick her up on my behalf, and I provided him with the necessary information.

When Lacey arrived, she immediately approached my room and inquired as to why she had change her calendar to include a flight to Virginia today. I told her to close the door, went into the safe, and pulled out the ticket, to which she responded, "Oh shit!" Stacey and I had been friends since our freshmen year in college. I was her maid of honor in her wedding, and she was maid of honor in my wedding. I was the godmother to her three children, and she was the godmother to all six of mine. First, let's turn in this ticket and get the check. Give Uncle Sam his share first, and you can keep the remaining amount as you plan to use this money for your own benefit. We proceeded as planned, and she made a phone call to the woman, informing her that she needed to see her today and that she was bringing a very important client with her. We went to the lottery office, and I turned in the winning ticket. I requested anonymity due to my fear that such a large sum of money would attract a diverse range of individuals. We left the lottery office and went to the accountant's office, where I met Delilah Brown-Hawkins. We talked for a long time about my plans for this money. I told her about the land. I intended to construct a structure on one section of the land and establish a productive farm on the other. The more I spent, the less taxes I paid, and she gave me ideas on how to spend. Her firm wrote checks that required two signatures and an explanation, including mine, to ensure I knew where my money was going.

When I called Daddy to ask if he was ready to sign over the land to me, he responded, "Girl, yeah, been ready." Now that I've retired, you can't imagine the financial burden it's been on me to consistently provide half of the monthly income since my retirement. I questioned why he hadn't informed me earlier; he explained that he wasn't aware of your financial situation due to your divorce and children attending college. I will reimburse you for all your expenses, including half of the taxes you have paid since your retirement. Yes, if you say so. That night, Stacy and I engaged in a lengthy conversation. I expressed my gratitude for the private detective's information, but I never had the chance to present it to her. We talked about the children and how they were dealing with the divorce; we just caught up on everything. The next day, we took her to the airport to see her off, and I hugged her and told her I would call her over the weekend.

I picked up my daddy, and we went to the city hall, where we handled all the paperwork. Now I am the owner of the land. I went to pick up Big Ma, and together we made our way to the land, praying for success. We lit the blessed sage to bless it. I made an appointment with the top three black architecture firms. They came to my house, and I explained what I wanted. The mansion, perched on a hill, has seven suites, each suite featuring three bedrooms, a walk-in closet for each bedroom, and a shared area. I need two elevators in the house, one for personal use and the other for emergency use in case the main elevator malfunctions. Additionally, I require a spacious baker's kitchen, a formal living room, a large den, a movie room, and a formal dining room. The house features a sunroom with screened-in porch for my suite, a screened-in porch at each end of the house, a playroom for the grandchildren, a fireplace in the den, two bathrooms for each suite, an inground pool with a gate, an outdoor kitchen, and a patio. The main road comes to the back and the front of the house, and a handicapped-accessible entrance is present. The same street is home to seven modest houses, each featuring three bedrooms, two complete bathrooms, and a spacious kitchen with a garage. We plan to construct a three-story employment apartment building that can accommodate thirty employees. Each floor will have ten rooms and a common area equipped with refrigerators and microwaves, as well as a full kitchen on the first floor. I plan to construct horse stables that can accommodate up to eight horses, although I'm not planning to buy so many, along with an entertainment facility for hosting events and gatherings. There will be an electronic gate around the entire estate with backup generators. I bought an escalator, and Lois, who was my driver until I hired one, accompanied me to the property to gain a better understanding of the terrain.

I'm going to make donations to my college and church, but I'll donate to the home church that all of my ancestors attended. The church cemetery holds the majority of my ancestors' graves. During slave days, the slaves sang, and they had a preacher preach to them in the yard of the slave quarter. After slavery ended, many of my ancestors continued to work on the farm as sharecroppers, as they had no knowledge of life outside the farm. Bercier permitted them to construct a modest structure, complete with benches, serving as a church and a school for reading instruction, as none of the former slaves had any formal education. When Bercier died in his will, he left fifty acres, and years later the family bought another fifty acres. They originally built Salem Southern Baptist Church on ten acres of the land they donated to the church. Because the majority of the young people had left the area or stopped attending, the congregation had dwindled in size. I overheard Big Ma discussing over the phone how they were struggling to pay their mortgage due to low income, the small congregation, and the lack of central heating and air conditioning. I paid off their mortgage and had a contractor go out and put in central heat and air. They had converted the church from a wood structure to a larger brick structure with a bell tower, and when it was time for service, someone would ring the bell, letting people know it was time for service.

I also wanted to buy houses and renovate them; some I would sell, others I would rent out to lower-income people in section eight. I will be opening my own business, McCray-Fontenot LLC, Inc. I decided to retire at the end of August to run my business. I will rent a conference room in a local hotel for the designers to conduct their presentation, and I have invited my lawyer, accountant, all of my children, and Lois to attend.

Now I have to tell my family about my fortune. One night I had dinner catered from Crab House. They were shocked to see all the food in the backyard, under the screen in the back porch, free of flies, and inquired about the occasion. I explained that with Bella and Ernest's impending departure, it would be a while before we could all have dinner together. I wanted to celebrate Ernest and Bella's new adventures, even though they were seventeen and their birthday was not until October. I pray they will follow the righteous path, and they will look out for each other. I have some exciting news to share with them. I am retiring from my job after twenty-seven years, and we would never worry about money again if we handled money right. I informed them that I was the only winner in the lottery. I didn't give them the amount I received. I informed them that only a select few were aware of it and instructed them to keep it a secret. It was the family secret.

They were shocked. After Lillian turns eighteen, I must sell this house and split the money with your father.

I am having a house built for us on the land I own. Big Ma and I blessed the land, and I'll be meeting with the designers in a couple of months. I wanted them to be there when they reviewed the designs.

Raymond had a look of doom on his face. I asked him what's wrong, and he announces he has a son. His college girlfriend was pregnant when they graduated, and she did not tell him because she thought he was going pro. This morning, he received a call informing him that she had given birth, threatening to place the child in foster care unless he travels to Houston to pick him up. I responded, "We don't give our babies away." Do you need me to go? He said yes.

CHAPTER 21

Becoming the ancestor

THE ANCESTORS GAVE ME SIGNS THAT DEATH WAS COMING. ONE morning, Shauna and I were eating breakfast. Shauna said, "Death is coming." I learned that seeing a cardinal indicated the presence of an ancestor, whereas hearing a hooting owl indicated the impending death. I listened, and yes, I heard it, but I tried to ignore it. I didn't have any trees in my yard, so I assumed it was a nearby tree. Shauna surprised me. She had more insight than I thought, and I asked her "what she meant by that." Shauna replied, "Someone is going to go to heaven." "How do you know this?" I asked, "Big Ma told me." Big Ma imparted extensive knowledge to Shauna, and she successfully retained most of it.

Later that night I get a call from Pricilla saying Marie had a heart attack and died before the rescue squad arrived. "Oh my God, I replied, How are Lamont and Donnell handling it? How is Jacque doing?" Donnell is currently doing well, but Lamont's is not improving. We have not talked to Jacque yet. Donnell and Lamont are leaving tomorrow morning at six. I have called my three older children, and they will meet us in Lake Charles. The two younger children and I will leave on Thursday, and Donnell will pick us up in Houston. On Saturday, they will provide services for her.

Let me text all my kids and see what they say. I sent a text to all my children, informing them about their grandmother. Regardless of how she treated us, we are God's children, and we will all attend and grow as individuals. Despite some opposition, all of my children decided to attend. I inquired with Bella and Gerald about their last class, and I, along with Lois, planned to drive up to collect them. I also sent an email to their coach, informing them that they would be departing on Wednesday and returning on the following Wednesday, as we would be in Louisiana due to their grandmother's death. Raymond informed administrators for Lillian and Gerald while he took a leave of absence. When I asked Lois if she wanted to go, she replied that she was going to rest while we were away. I asked her if she needed some help, and she said no, but she just wanted some quiet time.

Baby Blake was nine months old and growing like a weed daily. I secured reservations for eight seats in first class, ensuring that we could all sit together. Additionally, I arranged for a party bus to transport us to the airport and a nine-passenger SUV to transport us to Lake Charles, where we could accommodate a child's car seat. Finally, I secured a hotel with two suites, allowing us to spend three nights in Lake Charles and one night in Houston due to our early flight.

Pricilla left the day before us, and we arrived in Houston on Friday. When I called her, I inquired about her current residence, to which she replied, "The same place I always stay." I also inquired about her mood and the well-being of her siblings, to which she replied, "Okay." Your ex is here with Suzanne, and she is acting like she is the wife." "We don't want any trouble, I explained. We are going to show our support for Jacque because we all know that my children and I were not her favorites." Pricilla asked, "Did you bring Blake with his fat pretty self?" I replied, "Yes." "Aunt Faye is waiting for you, so hurry up and get here," she said, and I agreed. We arrived in Houston around ten that morning, after getting all the luggage, and Raymond went to pick up the vehicle I rented. We loaded up and went to Lake Charles.

After checking into the hotel around noon, Raymond, Gerald, and Ernest went to our favorite restaurant and got takeout for us all. After eating, we all went to sleep because we were tired. Blake woke me up around four, and I woke up everyone else and told them let's prepare to go see their grandfather.

When we pulled up, Pricilla saw me getting out of the car and came over to get Blake, but he would not go to her. "It's about time you get here, she stated." Getting up at three thirty and leaving for the airport at five exhausted us. We arrived around twelve, ate, and went to sleep. We now have a baby with us, which is a significant change." Aunt Faye came down and hugged all of us and said, "Let me have this fat baby," and by surprise, he went to her.

As we made our way to the porch, Suzanne noticed us, and Ernest and Bella positioned themselves in front of me, acting as a protective barrier. Suzanne approaches me, with Ernest and Bella standing in front of me, and asks, "Why are you here?" Marie hated you, and everyone knows it, because she did not hide it." Belle says, "Mama, please let me slap the shit out of this bitch, please." I replied, "Ignore her; that's what she wants," and we walked past her. Shauna sees Philip in the yard talking to some people and asking, "Can I go and speak to Daddy?" and I say yes. Lillian and Shauna approach Philip, saying "hi, Daddy," and he embraces them both as if he's truly missed them. When he sees the rest of the family, he walks over to the porch and engages in conversation with the other children. Despite their differences, it's clear that they still love each other. He notices Aunt Faye with Blake and inquiries about the young man's identity. She responds, "This is your grandson," and reaches out to him, prompting Blake to approach him. When Blake sees me, he gets fussy and reaches for me, so I take him. I ask Philip, "Where is your father?" and he replies that "he's in the living room with other family members," so we all head to the house to see Jacqu.

When we walk into the living room, he is shocked to see us and says, "I didn't think y'all were coming." I told him, You know, we were going to be here to support you. When he sees Blake, he says, "Is this my great-grandson?" and I say yes. Blake crawled up toward Jacque, who picked him up and played with him. Philip's siblings came in and hugged me, expressing their gratitude for my visit. Suzanne kept coming in and out, observing what I was doing. She was annoyed that Philip's siblings were so loving towards me, but she was not pleased that I was there.

Around ten, Blake began to fuss, so I gave him a bottle, laid him in my lap, and he fell asleep. Around eleven, I told Bella to get her siblings so we could get ready to go back to the hotel, and I told Aunt Faye that I would come over to her house with Pricilla in the morning. Friday was the viewing from twelve to five, and after that, we went to the house and back to the hotel by nine because tomorrow will be a busy day. As I was leaving, Philip took Blake from me so I could descend the steps. He said, "I need to talk to you and the kids in private; can I come by the hotel in an hour to talk to y'all?" to which I replied, "Yes."

When I get into the car and Bella straps Blake in his car seat, the first thing Raymond and Bella say is, "What did he say to you?" After telling them what he had said, Ernest responded, "There's nothing he can say; he chose who and what he wants; let the past be the past." I said no; you may not want to forgive your father now, but just listen to what he has to say. Bella says he better not bring that bitch with him. I said, "Bella, when did you start to use that type of language?" Seeing her makes me irritable all over again. "You can't put all the blame on her. Your father made this decision, understood the risks involved when he decided to engage with her, and was also influenced by external factors." Who" everyone questioned? "Marie," Gerald said. Ernest asked, Does anyone know about your financial blessing? Did you tell Aunt Pricilla? I said "no." I haven't told my own mama yet. You, my accountant, my lawyer, Big Ma, and your Godmother Lacey are the only ones who know. Well, let's just wait and see what he says before you draw your own conclusion. By the time Raymond had bathed Blake and I had put him in clean pajamas, Philip had called to ask where he wanted to meet. I gave him the number to my suite, and he came up.

The boys came to my room, and Raymond placed Blake in the travel crib. Philip says, "First, I want to apologize to you, Charlotte. You did not deserve the way I treated you. I am deeply sorry for not helping you with the children and for having an affair with Suzanne. You deserve so much more from me. Ernest I want to apologize for slapping you and Raymond. I want to apologize to you for what you saw. I want to apologize to you all for not being present for you when I was there. I want you to know I love my children, and please forgive me."

Bella said, "What about Mama?" Do you still love her?" Philip said I will always love your mama, but I am not in love with her. I am in love with Suzanne and have been for a long time." "How can you love a woman who allowed you to break up your family?" Bella asked? Every time you would sneak around with that woman while you were still with Mama, you allowed her to put a wedge between you and Mama's relationship. I can't forgive that easily; maybe I will one day, but not today." The other children agreed, but Shauna said, "I still love you, Daddy." "Do you realize how you hurt us?" Ernest asked. Over the past few years, we have not received any correspondence from you. We received no birthday cards for our birthdays, and you didn't attend any of Raymond's, Shauna's, Bella's, or my graduations. Philip responded, "I understand that what I've done is irreversible. Could you please grant me another opportunity?" Ernest replied, "You don't have your prize possessions to show off anymore. Everyone can clearly see your true nature. Why did you marry our mother if you were so in love with Suzanne? I am like Bella. I can't forgive you so easily; as a matter of fact, the sight of you makes me sick." Philip began to cry and said, "I want to be in Blake's life." Raymond said, "Hell no. I want to maintain a positive influence in his life, and you do not fit that description. We won't visit you and Suzanne in Houston, and we don't feel comfortable with you visiting us in Virginia because we don't trust you. With the voice of defeat, Philip says, "I understand. I will leave and hope to talk to y'all tomorrow. I know it's getting late, and we all have a busy day tomorrow."

After his departure, I expressed, "I sense a change in his behavior." Perhaps he discovered that the baby Suzanne has was not his own. Everybody says, "What baby?" "Suzanne has a daughter about eight, and he says that's his daughter, but it's not." "How do you know?" Gerald asked. "Don't worry, I know. I said. Let's get ready for bed; I'm tired." The boys said goodnight. When the girls were taking their showers, I gave Blake a bottle, and he fell asleep drinking it. Finally, I took a shower. I know I was asleep by eleven thirty.

When the family was lining up at the church, they asked for children. Pricilla said, "Come on up here with me." I shook my head and said no, preferring to stay with my children. The service was beautiful, but I noticed that there were very few tears shed by her children and grandchildren. After the repast, we hung around the house for a while, but we needed to go and rest because we were spending time with Jaque and Aunt Faye and giving the children time to hang out with their cousins. We will be returning to Virginia on Monday.

CHAPTER 22

· ·

Changes are coming!

By the first of October, I should be able to move into the finished house and the other buildings on the estate. I have hired various staff members for the house, including cooks, grounds men, maintenance men, a seasonal pool person who doubles as a lifeguard, stablemen, and security guards. I definitely needed security. I did background checks on everyone I employed and they all signed a non-disclosure,

Daddy had received numerous offers about buying the land after he won it. Even though the land was on the outskirts of the city, white folks didn't want black folks moving out there, especially black folks they could not control. I named my property Fontenot Estates; it had an electric fence around the whole property with a backup generator. I had to install an electronic fence to keep out intruders and wild animals, particularly wild hogs. They had infiltrated the county and posed a significant threat. They had the potential to not only destroy your property but also cause human casualties. I did not need that trouble.

All employees underwent background checks and signed a non-disclosure agreement because I protect my family's privacy. We will move some furniture from the old house to the new one, but we have also ordered a significant amount of new furniture. I make visits to the land twice a week, but I get daily photos of the progress. As a woman with no experience, I ensure proper completion of tasks by walking around with the builder to prevent any potential shortcuts that could negatively impact us later. My trustworthy friend, an inspector, inspects everything for me. If he finds any errors, he informs me, we arrange a meeting with the builder, and the builder is required to make corrections at their own expense.

Ernest and Bella have graduated; Gerald is off to college. I gave him the option to attend any HBCU he wanted, but he felt that he would keep the family tradition by attending the same college as everyone else in the family. Bella is married to a man in the army named Scott Larue. She got married because she was pregnant, and I reminded her she did not have to marry him. I truly don't like the young man. I was aware of the ongoing events, and one day I went to visit Bella, informing her that the ancestors were visiting me nightly and that this individual was not suitable for her. But before I visited her, Ernest came home one weekend, and I asked him who he was and what he knew about him. I promised I would not let Bella know we talked. He began to tell me that he had tried to talk to Bella about him. He was known as a skirt chaser around campus. He is in the army, stationed at a base close to campus. When I first met him along with the rest of the family, I didn't like the way he looked at Shauna and Lillian. I told him that I didn't like him; I conducted a background check on him and found that he was from a small town near Mobil, Alabama, and that he had joined the military because he had gotten a white girl pregnant, for which the girl's family had threatened to kill him. He had done well for an enlisted soldier; his biggest downfall was chasing women. I didn't like the way he treated Bella, because she spent more time at my house alone than at her apartment with him. One night, when we were alone, I asked her, Was he treating her right? She was aware that I already knew the answer. She always had a look of hurt on her face. I explained to her that if she was unhappy, she always had a home to come too.

Philip called because he is trying to develop a relationship with the children, but I think it's too late. Most of the time, they refuse to answer or return his calls. When he calls, he tells me how he is trying to repair the relationship but the children won't return his calls. One night, he became frustrated and said, "I want the children all to myself, which is why I won't help." I reminded him that if he had stepped up as a father during the formative years, he would not have had the problems he is currently facing.

Joe and I are still friends, we spend our extra time together, but he has children at home as well. We spend a lot of time on the phone. After I move I want us to take a trip to the Bahamas, just the two of us.

I noticed that Big Ma was moving slower as each day go by. When I picked her up for her Wednesday shopping, she reminded me that today was her doctor's appointment, and this time she wanted me to go in with her and speak with her doctor, she has never wanted that before. When we went into the exam room, she got undressed so the doctor could examine her, after we went in his office to talk to him. He asked her a lot of questions about how she is feeling, and that the cancer had spread from the last test, and he would give her three to six months. I'm looking confused. What cancer? What test I asked. Dr. Snead stated that my Big Ma has leukemia, and she refused treatment. "{Why did you refuse treatment I asked looking at Big Ma?" I am surprised she has lasted this long the doctor said. "My herbs and God Big Ma said. I am eighty-nine years old. I don't want those chemicals going through my body, being hooked up to a pole for three and four hours, losing my hair, the chemicals burning my insides, I am not having nothing to do with it she stated. When my time comes, I am ready. I have lived a good life." Tears are streaming down my cheeks, I feel like the air has been sucked out of my lungs.

When we got to the car she said "Baby girl, stop that crying. You knew this day would happen, you have been ignoring the signs from the ancestor's that's why I wanted you to go with me and talk to the doctor. I have lived a good life, God has blessed me. I have made my peace a long time ago and I am ready to have a seat amongst the ancestors. I have prepared you, now it's your time to be the head of Sarah's Daughters, everyone knows what is expected of them, if they decide to use their gift for evil, the ancestors will handle them. Like I taught you, you will have to teach the younger generation. Many are not using their blessing and are not teaching the young'uns the history of our blessing, some feels it's a curse, and others are using it for ill gains. We must continue to teach so there is an understanding, like I did you." "I am going to talk to Carol and see if she will allow me to teach her girls next summer.

I want you to come and stay with me Big Ma I said, No, to many things going on in your house. Two babies, and where am I going to sleep she asked. I will after you move into the new house, regardless of what the doctors said, I am going to bless those houses, and burn sage to rid of any demons. With all those people working on those grounds, you don't know what types spirits they have, and you don't need evil spirits lurking around the house and on the land." I told her "I am hiring around the clock care for her until I move into the house, and I will not take no for an answer."

We moved into the house a month earlier, I did a walk thru and Big Ma blessed the property, and each house along with my parents, siblings, and children. We toured the grounds, my kitchen staff fixed a delicious spread, and we just had a ball. When we moved in so did Big Ma, and my parents. My parents moved into the closest house to my house. I didn't want to leave them in their house because they were both in their mid-seventies. They sold their house and put the proceeds in a trust for their grandchildren. I moved Big Ma in the house with me and her bedroom was next to mine. She had three full-time nurses that worked Monday thru Friday, eight-hour shifts, and three part-time nurses that worked only on the weekend. They too had to sign a non-disclosure because I needed to protect my family, I also did background check before they started working with her.

Early in March Big Ma had summoned her ministers, from North Carolina, and from Virginia. She told them that "her days on this earth is coming to an end, but there were some things she needed to talk to them. She told the pastor from North Carolina she had always paid her tides in both places, but he was young and did not really know her, and that she wanted her paster in Virginia to preach her eulogy and hoped it would not be a problem for him. She told him she wanted the old spirituals she was raised on sung for her service. I want to be buried in the church cemetery along with my parents and the other ancestors, furthermore it's already paid for. I know you have heard things about me and other females in my family. I want you to hear it from me and you can come to your own conclusion of me. Either of you have a heaven or hell to put me in, what I am about to tell you is between me, you and God, Babygirl already know. I know you have heard rumors that I'm a root woman, hoodoo woman, witch, I put roots on people. I have never harmed a soul.

In the late 1700's a slave woman named Sarah was captured in Africa, and against her will she was bought to America in the belly of a slave ship. Sarah was the name given by her first master, had dreams, in her dreams the old ancestors told her things that was about to happen, and she was taught from a little girl how roots and herbs worked as medicine. Out of fear she only practice her gift in secret but after Bercier became her new master she practiced her medicine, by healing slaves, delivering babies, and even some white folks because remember white doctors did not treat slaves. Sarah taught her daughters, and this blessing has been passed down from generation to generation.

Now some of the women have used their gift for evil and to make a profit, they have to answer for their doing, not I. The medicine I make is to help people. Then she looked at her minister from Virginia, remember the medicine I sent you when you came down with covid I told you to take a table spoon every four hours and to eat the soup I prepared.

Did you use it? Remember I know when you are lying. I helped people before this covid had a name or a cure. The ancestors warned me and told me to prepare for this about three years before the pandemic. I did! Many of the women don't practice their gift, many were forbidden. They were told it was evil and going against God.

People don't realize when the slaves came to America they served God, but not the way white's did. Whites transferred their dislike to the slaves.

She began to deteriorate early one morning on April 6, prompting us to call the rescue squad. Upon our arrival at the hospital, the doctor informed us that she might not survive the week. I called Mama, Aunt Francis, and Carol and told them what was going on, and they needed to get here no later than tomorrow. That night, I was sitting by her bed, resting my head on it, and she noticed my tears. She rubbed my head and said, "As the days go by, you won't cry for me as much." I assured Big Mama that my heart would cry for her. That evening Bella, Shauna, Lillian, and Mama came up to the room. We put her in her lavender caftan, which I had cut down the middle of the back to make it easier to dress her, and placed tea lights around the room. We turned out the lights over her head because time was getting near. Aunt Francis, her daughter Shay, and Shay's daughter Zion came into the room soon after, as did Carol and her girls Yolanda and Maurice. I crawled into bed with her, and everyone in the room touched a different part of her body as she began to transition to the softly playing song "Ship of Zion." Her breathing was getting shallow, and as she took her last breath, she turned her head and looked at me, smiling. April 8, 2011, 9:28 p.m. I watched as her spirit left her body. I checked for a pulse, and there was none. We all held hands, and as tears streamed down my face, I said, "God of all God's, God of our ancestors, here lies your daughter Tilda." She was the daughter of Cassie, Bessie, Elizabeth, Winnie, Bell, Fannie, and Sarah. Accept her into your kingdom, along with the ancestors. As I said, "She is now with the ancestors." We called the nurse and declared her dead. We bathed her and wrapped her in a white winding sheet. We all went back to my house. Aunt Francis stayed with Mama and Daddy; Carol, Shay, and their daughters stayed with me. I will contact the funeral home in the morning.

I called Joe while leaving the hospital, and he said he would meet me at the house. I contacted Gerald and informed him that I would notify Ernest and Raymond once I arrived home. After we got home, we raided the refrigerator because we were all hungry. Shay and Carol were asking me a lot of questions about what I did at the hospital. Like Mama, Aunt Francis did not practice her blessing, which instilled fear in both Shay and Carol. Carol asked how you were able to learn the old ways and practice your blessing. I explained to her I spent a lot of time with Big Ma. When I was younger, Big Ma told me that I was the one who would continue to practice the old ways, much like Sarah. Shay mentioned that I wanted to have boys; that way I would not have to deal with the situation, but as my daughter grew older and began to ask me questions about elderly women talking to her while she slept, I became fearful. When I attempted to discuss the situation with Mama, she advised me not to bring up such a sensitive topic.

Carol's revelation that Mama knew she was having sex in high school terrified me. Remember the time when we experienced severe menstrual cramps and Mama had a homemade medicine that she would administer to us? Mama didn't make it; Big Ma did. She would make about twelve bottles a year and give them to family members for their daughter's cramps. I assisted her, and as she grew older, she kept a book filled with instructions on how to make specific medicines, prayers, plants, and use of herbs, among other things.

I showed them a locked closet filled with a variety of items I had made, as well as the herbs I grew on my private patio outside my bedroom. "Why do you let your mother's fear scare you?" I asked. Carol said, "I thought I was too old to learn now." How are your daughters handling their gifts? Carol said she knew that her daughter Casandra would have dreams of the future. What do you tell her? I explained to her that the devil was manipulating her thoughts, just as my mother had always done. Come here with your girls the week after the Fourth of July; let's just talk, and I will teach you some of the old ways, demonstrating that their blessings are not a curse, or that the devil is not manipulating them, or that they are not insane.

That night Joe stayed with me, and I cried like a baby. He just held me. I made all the arrangements the next day. I rented two chauffeured limo buses from the funeral home so that no one had to drive; it took all my family, my parents, and three of my mother's cousins; all the family wore white, including the men of the family, and I had two hundred and fifty lapel pins made with a tiny lavender bulb wrapped in a lavender ribbon.

Lavender flowers draped her casket. All family members wore white. The men donned white suits, while the women donned white dresses. At the end of the service, the family had their final viewing. My children cried in a way I had never seen before. I came to the realization that Big Ma, was the other grandmother my children never had.

I was the last one to view her. I leaned over and kissed her for the last time. After the funeral director lowered her into the casket, I placed the blanket over her. The funeral director assisted me in closing the casket. The funeral director and his assistant rolled her body to the door and, using the pall barriers, which consisted of her nephews and great-nephews, carried her to her final resting place at the back of the church. We sat under the tent as the minister delivered his final remarks, stating, "Matilda Francis Jasper-Weaver "You were God's servant. You helped take care of the sick, fed the hungry, and clothed those who needed clothes. Regardless, you helped those in need with a smile on your face, and you never complained. You ran a good race, and your work is done. May your soul rest in peace.

Bella has always had a beautiful voice, belting out, "Sit down, servant, sit-down, sit-down servant, sit-down, sit-down servant, sit down, sit down, and rest a little while." As everyone began to sing the chorus, Bella continued, "I know you tired, sit down, I know you tired, sit down, I know you tired, sit down, and rest a little while." While everyone started to depart, I remained seated. It was heartbreaking to leave her in a box, lowered into the ground next to her mother's grave. I heard her whisper in my ear, "Get up, walk around, and look at the history of Sarah's daughters."

CHAPTER 23

....

I'm Exhausted

I WAS UNAWARE OF THE LARGE NUMBER OF ATTENDEES AT THE funeral until I arrived for the re pass. Many people attended the funeral from Virginia, where her church had rented two thirty-six passenger buses. Joe's sister and two of his children arrived in the limousine I had rented.

Some of my former neighbors were present, including one of my best friends, Lacey and her husband Mark, as well as my in-laws, Pricilla, Donnell, and Lamont. However, Philip's presence was the most shocking revelation. We decided not to let the babies go, so Miss Judy kept them at the pastor's house next door to the church. We would not feed anyone until the immediate family arrived. When I came in and sat down, the ushers started serving food. I ate a little and went around talking to family and friends. Lacy asked, "Are you ok?" "I said no, I'm exhausted, but after today I am going home and staying in bed for a couple of days." I asked her. Can you take off a week? The week after Ernest's wedding?" Why ? Lacy inquired. "A five-day, four-night stay in Aruba" "I'm game; who else is coming?"

"I am inviting Pricilla, Carol, Lois, and my cousin Shay. We will enjoy rest and relaxation, private suites, massages, food, unlimited alcohol, and beachside rooms where we can converse and enjoy ourselves. Having fun is something I'm missing. However, now that Gerald has his degree, he is going to take classes to get his master's next semester. He works at the Delilah Brown-Hawkins accounting firm, which allows him to closely monitor my finances. Bella will complete her masters in December. Lillie is in her junior year; I'm almost done. That gave me hope. I call Pricilla, Lois, Shay, and Carol over; does everyone have a passport? They replied yes. I told them the details the week after Ernest's wedding. They all agreed that they wanted to go. Lacy and Carol said they would drive down together, and Shay said she would drive down too, since I don't live near you. We could all leave my house together.

Pricilla said, "Girl Philip looked like he wanted to blow a gasket when he saw Joe walk in the church with you holding his hand. He leaned over to Donnell and asked who was that man, and Donnell told him it was your friend Joe. Then he asked, "What kind of friend is Joe?" Donnell said, "I don't know; ask her." "Yes, it's because he is jealous," I replied. Who cares, I asked. We all burst out laughing.

The next thing I knew, Philip worked his way over to where I was and reached out to hug me, and I backed away. I thanked him for coming. I understand the deep affection your Big Ma had for you and the kids, and I wanted to extend my support, just as you did when Mama passed away. Why didn't you tell me that Bella was married and had two kids?" Philip asked. This is not the time or place to discuss the children, I replied. Well, you've got an opportunity to talk to them now. I looked at him and walked away. As people began to leave, I was ready to leave, but I didn't want to leave her here. I walked to the back of the church, kissed the tip of my fingers on the mound of dirt that now covered her, and walked away, this time not looking back. When we got in the bus to leave, I sat next to Joe, laid my head on his shoulder, and cried as the bus pulled away. Raymond reached over and touched my shoulder.

I heard the kids talking about their daddy. He had the opportunity to see Bella's children and remarked to Bella that Anya resembled her in her early years. Bella said, "Were you around when I was a baby?" "That's why Mama had to hire Lois because she needed help. Gerald replied. Philip's face expressed his disapproval without uttering a single word. He asked Robert and Bella to please send him photos of the babies. They agreed. I fell asleep for an hour and woke up as we approached the gate. I got me something to eat, took a mild sedative, and I was out.

When I finally woke up, I felt a persistent kicking sensation in my back. I turned over, and there was baby Anya kicking and smiling. I reached over and said, What are you doing in here, baby girl? Then I remembered that baby girl was the name Big Ma called me. I reached over and grabbed my phone and called Bella. When she answered, I asked, Why is baby Anya in my bed? This morning, after getting her up, changing her, feeding her, and putting her clothes on, she began to cry. As I was leaving her to go to the nanny, Lois called me to come get her, suspecting that something was wrong with her. I checked her temperature and found it was normal, but when we walked past your room, she would stop. However, when she realized we weren't going into your room, she would start up again. So, I grabbed my laptop, entered your room, laid her next to you, and she curled up and went back to sleep. When I left, she was already asleep, and I didn't stay away for more than a few minutes before heading to the bathroom. I approached her and lifted her up. "Would you like to play with your grandmother?" I inquired. She responded by grinning and drooling, as she was experiencing teething. Finally, she returned to the nanny.

I grabbed the phone and called Joe. "Good morning," I said. I just want to say thank you for being there for me through the toughest times in my life. You were there for me when Blake was born, dropping everything to travel with me to Houston, and pushing Big Ma in the wheelchair down the boardwalk at the beach. You have been a life savior for me, and you just don't know how much I appreciate it." "What are you doing, he asked?"? "I'm lying here in this bed and getting some rest." Joe replied, "You need it; I will call you later."

As I lay in bed, I remembered what Big Ma said— you got to teach the young'uns. I called Shay and asked, "What are you doing?" Nothing sitting here looking busy. Shay replied. A lot of people in my office are on vacation. I asked her if she could come up the week after July 4 and bring Zion. She said that's no problem. You won't believe it, but last night, I received numerous calls from many of our female family members. They were discussing how you had incorporated many of the traditional practices into the services, which we were the only ones aware of. Additionally, there were others who were interested in learning about our gifts that were previously off-limits.

Text me their names and numbers, and I will give them a call to see where their head is. All of them are cousins; some I talked to occasionally at funerals and family reunions. There were two cousins that I was unfamiliar with, but once they revealed their identity, I came to understand who they were. They began to tell me how they were forbidden to even go around family members who practiced and made to believe that it was root work. I decided to invite them all to my home and teach them about our family history of Sarah, who were the ancestors and why they came to you, the meaning of the color lavender, signs and what their meanings are, the burning of sage and ridding your house of evil spirits, keeping evil spirits from entering your house, how to talk to your girls and explain it to them, never cease from praying, and using herbs for medicine. It would be interesting.

CHAPTER 24

....

My children are adult's

I KNEW ERNEST AND TRUDY WOULD MARRY SOON AFTER graduation. Trudy did not return to her native New York; she said she grew up in a place that is always busy, and she loved the calmness of the south. When she graduated, an accounting job awaited her, and she had already secured admission into the master's program in Hampton. Yea, it cost more, but it's better than trying to go to Norfolk two times a week. A year after their graduation, they exchanged vows in the college chapel. The chapel is beautiful; it always had beautiful stained-glass windows. During my four years here, I remember coming to church on Sundays.

I met Trudy's parents the night I hosted the rehearsal dinner in Richmond. Trudy's grandmother grabbed my hand and said, "You are special." I'm Haitian, I know and smiled. My grandbaby is in good hands. Richmond restaurants had more to offer; my assistant, Shakira, found four restaurants about nine months before the wedding, and we made appointments to go there and sample their food. Prior to her death, Big Ma, Lois, Shakira, Lillie,

Shauna, and myself did a food tasting, and we rated each sample after dinner and placed it in a sealed envelope after every food tasting. At the end of the month, I tallied each restaurant, and we decided to go with a restaurant called The Chiale. It covered a lot of varieties. I had a contract for forty people, so that evening I had a party bus to transport those of us to Richmond for the dinner, and it was a beautiful dinner.

Trudy's colors were navy and cream. Bridesmaids wore navy gowns, and groomsmen wore navy tuxes with cream shirts. Flowers were navy and white. Ernest was wearing a blue tux and a blue vest. I wore a navy tool gown and a sheer waist-length jacket. All of my children were at the wedding. Bella and Lillian served as bridesmaids, Shauna carried Big Ma's photo as a tribute to her, and Trudy's niece carried a photo of her grandfather as a tribute to him. On the night of the rehearsal dinner, Ernest pulled his Papa Jacque aside and explained the importance of honoring the ancestors. He decided not to honor Marie, as she had never been a grandmother to him, and hoped he understood. Jacque asked, "Are you too old for your old grandpa to hug and kiss?" He responded, "No," and they both laughed.

The day of the wedding. I arranged for Ernest to meet me and Trudy at the bridal suite's door, along with her parents. I instructed Trudy to stick her hand out of the door with her back turned, and I instructed Ernest to turn his back to the door so he wouldn't see her. I then prayed for them, just as Big Ma had done for me. When we arrived at the church, Jacque, Aunt Faye, and other siblings of Philips were already present. His aunts, Pricilla and Carol, and his uncles, Darnell and Lamont, were also present, as were my siblings, my parents, and many of his cousins. Joe and his family also attended, but Philip did not receive an invitation. During the wedding procession, Ernest escorted me down the aisle, kissed me on the cheek, and said, "Thank you, mama, I love you." I broke down in tears because he was the first of my children I witnessed getting married.

A Catholic priest married Ernest and Trudy, and they chose the Hollywood Hotel Ballroom in Richmond for their reception, which hosted three hundred guests. The atmosphere was full of love, and the food was delicious. Trudy had a lot of Haitian dishes, as well as a lot of southern dishes. We danced and partied until one in the morning. The young folks party much harder than we did back in the day. It was fortunate that many of us had hotel rooms, as the alcohol was plentiful. It was a beautiful day and occasion. Three months later, they announce they are pregnant with their first child. Thank you, God, for allowing me to see this day and bringing a new daughter into my family.

CHAPTER 25

Rest and relaxation

THE NIGHT OF THE WEDDING, MY ANCESTORS WARNED ME THAT trouble was on the horizon. Be ready because trouble is coming. I thought that I would never rest for the things that were happening in my life. The following week, Joe and his family went on vacation, and that's one of the reasons I decided to take a girl's trip with Carol, Pricilla, Shay, Lois, and Lacy.

Gerald is pursuing an internship, allowing him to monitor my finances during my absence. We left at three thirty that morning for Richmond, and our flight left at six and arrived in Miami at seven thirty. Our flight changed in Miami, and we had a two-hour layover, so we ate breakfast and took a straight flight to Aruba. When we arrived, I had arranged for a limo to pick us up and take us to the resort. Our suites were beautiful, and our rooms on the beach had balconies. We arrived by three that afternoon, and we all decided to change and go to the pool to have a swim and relax. We ate dinner that evening and went to see an R&B legend perform that night.

Every morning, we ate breakfast in my room to discuss the activities for that day. Everyone wanted to go shopping today, and that was what we did. I would buy mostly clothes for the grandchildren, a dress or two that I thought my daughters would like, and t-shirts for the boys and Joe. When we returned, we went horseback riding in the ocean, and that was scary because I didn't realize we would be going in such deep water. When we returned, I rented a cabana where we lay by the beach, had drinks, and ate sandwiches. We showered and had dinner at a resort restaurant after returning to our rooms. We went to see a Jamaican band perform, and before we knew it, it was one in the morning. Time goes by fast when you are having fun.

The following day, we visited the spa, and my body felt remarkably rejuvenated. We visited the beach and enjoyed some leisurely time. Subsequently, we dined out and resolved to unwind that evening. We would gather in my room and engage in conversation. As I was taking a shower in my room, I called Bella and Lillian to inquire if their ancestors were visiting them at night. Both of them confirmed that they were. They asked me why. Was I okay? I told them I was good, asked how their sister and brothers were, and they said everything was going well. I said I would see them in a couple of days.

Before we knew it, it was time to head back to the states. We took many photos, looking like we'd just left the sun. This morning, upon entering my room, everyone had this expression on their faces, prompting me to inquire about the situation. Pricilla texted me the link, and as we sat down to eat breakfast, I read the article. Philip faced arrest for embezzlement, money laundering, operating a

Ponzi scheme, and concealing funds in the Cayman Islands. He was looking at fifty years to life in federal prison. He was under a million-dollar bond. I asked Pricilla what she knew; she said she got the call last night, but it was too late to tell me. Where is Suzanne? She is playing victim, and she can't understand why Philip was doing this. Bullshit, I said. Philip is an adulterous ass, but he is not a thief. Something doesn't sound right. Jacque is trying to make bail by using his land. I was going to call him right now and tell him to hold off until I got back, and I did.

I texted my private investigator and sent him a copy of the news article, letting him know that I would be returning late tonight and asking him to gather as much information as possible for me. He texted OK. After breakfast, we made our way to the lobby for check-out, loaded our limo, and headed to the airport. We arrived in Richmond at seven that evening, and we were at our front gate by eight thirty. Return to reality and life. Although my body has rested, my mind remains occupied.

CHAPTER 26

....

You got to lay in the bed you made

MY KIDS WERE RELIEVED TO HAVE ME HOME, AND SO WERE Mama and Daddy. I instructed everyone to grab a bite to eat, and once we sat down at the table, I realized they all understood the situation. I said, "Talk to me, children. Should we help your father?" I explained that I had spoken to your grandfather, who was planning to use his farm to raise money for a bond and a lawyer, but I didn't think he should. They all agreed with me. Bella, Ernest, and Raymond didn't want their grandfather to do that.

Gerald and Lillian said they did not believe it. Everyone was curious about Suzanne's whereabouts, and I responded by saying 'she is playing the victim'. No one said anything. Here's the situation: your Papa Jacques is going to get a loan on his farm to help your father. He has never had to use his farm as a loan for anything, so I will take whatever necessary steps to prevent him from mortgaging his property. Raymond said, "Mama, I know you, and you will do whatever you feel is right, so it's up to you."

I have set aside two hundred and fifty thousand from the sale of the house. He never got his half. Everyone went to bed, except my crew, who I returned with. They looked at me and said, What are you going to do? Jacque has worked long and hard for his farm, and I don't want him to lose what has been in his family for generations. I asked Pricilla if any of the Fontenot children had ever had trouble before. No, she replied.

Finally I went to bed, and as I slept, Big Ma came to me and said, He is guilty of stupidity, but not of the charges against him. She then said, "Help him." Why? This man ripped my heart out of my chest. I don't trust people other than family anymore. Yes, you do. You trust those who work for you, Lois, and many others in your life. Don't let bitterness prevent you from helping those in need, especially Philip, who is in dire need of your assistance. He will be a part of you for the rest of your life. He is your children's father and grandfather. You may not be in love with him, but you still love him. You have the opportunity to assist him, so strive to be a better person. You will be blessed. I went back to sleep.

I knew Jacque rose early in the morning, so I called him. I told him don't try to use his farm; I am in the process of getting him a lawyer and getting him out on bail. He can't get out until his preliminary hearing, and hopefully everything will be in place. However, please keep the details of his lawyer's and bail payments confidential. He said OK.

I called my lawyer early that morning and told her to call me back ASAP. When she did, I told her that I needed the best criminal lawyer Texas has. "What's going on?"

she asked. "I'll send you the text." As soon as she opened the text, she exclaimed, "Damn!" "This time, he has gotten himself into a shitload of trouble." I knew he wasn't perfect; he was an adulterer, but he doesn't believe in illegal criminal activity. This has Suzanne's name all over it, and she is playing the innocent victim. They live together, so he can't live where she does. He just bought a new condo, so he will have to move in it alone. Give the lawyer as much information as possible and have them call me ASAP.

While waiting for the lawyer to call, I called Joe and explained everything that was happening, including my intentions and the reasons behind them. Joe said okay, but you don't have to explain anything to me. I told him I did, because we had a special relationship, and I could not do anything without him being aware of the situation and what my intentions are. He said, "If you feel you are doing what is best for Jaque, I will not question it." I inquired about dinner tonight, to which he agreed.

About three hours later, a lawyer by the name of Solomon H. Wiggins called me. "I have been reading about this case, and it is a tough case, but all the cases I take are tough cases," the lawyer said. "What are your acquittal statistics, I asked?" "Ninety-eight percent," he replied. "How much should I wire you?" Just send two hundred and fifty thousand, and after the preliminary, I will fax you the financial breakdown. I said okay. Now he is living with the state's main witness, and he can't, am I correct? He said yes. When you speak with him, inquire about the furnishing of his new condo and inform him that you must remove all his possessions from the house with Suzanne. He said I will handle that today, but do not tell him who is financing his bail and his fee. His preliminary hearing is tomorrow at nine; I will wire you the money today. Ok, he said.

I've got a private detective named Francis J. Tillery who will contact you. He is the best money can buy. He's already on the job, and he'll contact you as soon as I text him your information.

When I called Jacque to reassure him that everything was in order, he announced that he was leaving tonight with Aunt Faye and Philip's brother, Jacque Jr. God is going to bless you, daughter. He is blessing me every day, I said. The following day I got a call about noon that Philip was released on bond, and he is to go nowhere near Suzanne. Everyone entering the building was required to present identification and sign their name. She was on the banned list and had a restraining order in place. She is the devil's ally, and she will stop at nothing to protect herself and the other members she previously collaborated with.

Philip knew about this attorney, knew he couldn't afford him, and wanted to know who was paying him. At first, Philip believed that Suzanne was the one paying for him. However, Wiggins had to clarify that Suzanne was actually the reason he was in this situation; she was a witness for the federal government. I was informed that he remained in denial until the first day of his trial preparation, refusing to cooperate with his lawyer. When his lawyer showed him the evidence that Suzanne had turned to the federal government, it hit him like a ton of bricks; he had been used all the time as the fall guy. He plunged into a profound depression, frequently refusing to answer his phone or eat, to the extent that Jacque and Faye chose to remain by his side until the trial concluded, as he couldn't leave the state. Philip realized that he had lost the most important person in the world to him before Suzanne reentered his life, Charlotte. His children lost respect for him, which hurt him most.

His siblings had lost the closeness they once shared, and he blamed himself for allowing a woman to manipulate him and alienate himself from his family. He lost everything important, except his father and Aunt Faye. The trial lasted for six weeks. The government called twenty witnesses, presenting documents signed by Philip. Wiggins called ten witnesses, including Philip. It took approximately three weeks to find the final witness, but my keen eye detective managed to uncover her, so I remained unfazed; eventually, she was located.

Philip's secretary, Lorretta L. Jamison, had every document that Philip signed. Lorretta L. Jamison displayed documents that Philip had signed six months prior to his partnership with Suzanne, that was forged due to being active military duty at that time. Lorretta explained how she had to give him forms to sign so that he really didn't know what he was signing. Many of the forms had been falsified, and she demonstrated that he was absent from the office on the days when the majority of the transactions took place. Following the presentation of all the evidence, the judge dismissed all charges and issued a warrant for the arrest of Suzanne and her father. Philip shed tears and made the decision to move to Lake Charles with Jacque for approximately a month. He then returned to Houston, sold his condo, and stored his belongings in Lake Charles. Ultimately, he concluded that

Houston was not the right place for him and relocated back to Lake Charles. Before Philip permanently left Houston, he visited Lorretta and expressed his gratitude for everything she had done to support him. He returned to Lake Charles the next day.

CHAPTER 27

Moving Forward

PHILIP STAYED IN LAKE CHARLES FOR ABOUT SIX MONTHS, BUT could not find a job that challenged him, plus everyone knew about his trial and Suzanne so he decided to move back to Virginia and got a job with the school system as the district ROTC supervisor and decided to try to make amends with his children. He called the children several times, but none of them returned his call, so he asked his brothers where I lived, they gave him directions to the estate, I heard she built a house on her father's land, his brother said yea, she sure did and smiled.

Upon his initial arrival, the gated area and the presence of guards astonished him. However, the sight of Fontenot Estates directly in front of the gate heightened his astonishment, requiring the guards to summon permission from the house before he could enter the grounds. I allowed him to be on the estate, welcomed him into my home, and asked him if he wanted a cup of coffee. He replied yes; I had Fran bring out two cups of coffee and invited him out on the back porch. I told him that he had lost weight but looked OK for what he had gone through, and he said thanks.

I informed him that everyone is working, and because they live in the house, he needed to call before coming over again. Subsequently, he started bombarding me with numerous questions. Why did you lock your hair? What is that purple dot on your forehead? Who was that man with you at Big Ma's funeral? Where did you get money for all of this? I looked at him and said, "I owe you no explanation." You can leave after you finish your coffee, but please remember to call before coming over the next time.

At dinner, I told the kids that Philip had come over, and from now on he would have to call before dropping by. Later, he called me and inquired about the whereabouts of his half of the proceeds from the house sale. I reminded him that the money had gone to the lawyer and his bond, and he responded, "So, it was you that paid for my lawyer and bond." I informed him that I deducted your half of the house sale, covered your bond, and transferred the remaining funds to your lawyer. I took this action to prevent Jacque from obtaining a loan for his farm, as he owed me one hundred and fifty thousand dollars, which was my share of the funds. He replied that you have more than enough money. I thought to myself that he still hadn't learned.

CHAPTER 28

Birthing Babies

THE SITUATION WAS DIFFERENT WHEN EACH GRANDCHILD WAS born. I have been blessed. I was in the delivery room when all of my grandchildren, except Blake, were born. The day I told the children about winning the lottery, Raymond had a look on his face; actually, he looked puzzled. I asked him, "Are you okay?" No, I have a son. By whom I said? I knew he had been dating a young lady in college for a couple of years. Raymond claims he didn't know she was pregnant until she was six months along. She had assumed he was going to be a professional basketball player, and when he decided he wasn't going pro, it was late in the pregnancy.

He received a call from the hospital where she delivered the baby, urging him to come to Houston as soon as possible. I asked him, "Can you handle this, or do you need me to go?" He responded, "I need you to go with me, mama." I called Joe and asked if he was interested in a five-day trip to California, to which he replied, "Yes, come over and I will tell you about this trip, but I have something else to talk to you about." I informed my family lawyer about the situation, providing her with details about the birth and hospital records. I explained I wanted a DNA test first; she agreed, and as soon as we find out if Raymond is the father, we will take steps from there. Where is the mother? She is still in the hospital, but she stated that she does not want a child, and if it is Raymond's, I want to make sure that she can never get custody of him.

We will raise him. My lawyer informed me that she has a friend who practices family law, and she will reach out to him immediately. This young woman needs to give up her parental rights, she replied. I agreed with her. He will be the new addition to the Fontenot family. After arriving in Houston and checking into the hotel, we went straight to the hospital.

Carolyn, Blake's mother, stated that the only reason she got pregnant was because she knew she was going to be a professional basketball wife and Raymond was going to marry her. However, once he decided not to go pro, it was too late for her to get an abortion. My intentions were to put him up for adoption, but a nurse convinced me to inform Raymond, and I did. She refused to form a bond with the baby, issued strict directives to avoid bringing him into her room, and threatened to place him in foster care for adoption if Raymond declined.

The lawyer met us at the hospital, and he initially wanted a DNA test done to make sure he was a Fontenot, but I knew this beautiful baby boy looked just like his father as a newborn. I had newborn photos of all my children in my wallet, and I showed them to Joe, who agreed. The following day, the DNA results confirmed Raymond's paternity, prompting me to urge her to relinquish her parental rights. In order to prevent her from accusing anyone of bribery or intimidation, The procedure was recorded. The lawyer, a nurse, a social worker, and a doctor were in the room. The lawyer explained to her the details of giving up her parental rights, emphasizing that she could not change her mind once she signed the papers. She said, "Don't worry, I won't," before asking where to sign, which she did. Both the social worker and the doctor witnessed the signing. The lawyer confirmed that everything was in order, and we were now free to pick up baby Fontenot. The social worker inquired about the baby's name; Raymond was unsure, so I suggested Blake Ernie Fontenot and provided the address for sending the birth certificate and parental rights information. I asked Blake's mother would she like to see him before we leave; she said no. I thanked Mr. Weinstein, the lawyer, and all who assisted.

Pampers, a car seat, a stroller, and some other things that I will need to use until I get back to Virginia. When we went to the nursery to get Blake, I asked what type of milk he was given and how well was he handling the milk and they said good. He was a big baby, he weighed eight lbs., nine oz's, a head full of black curly hair. That night in the hotel he woke up once and after feeding and changing he had no problem going back to sleep. I wrapped him in the special blanket I had made, I would have to put his name on it when I get home.

We did not take giving birth lightly, and it was a beautiful occasion. One thing we did not do was lay in bed during labor and delivery. We did a lot of walking, assisting the mother. We also squatted on the side of the bed, with the assistance of the midwife, doula, and doctor.

That was helpful when giving birth. When preparing for the birth of Isaac, Bella did not want her husband in the room with her. As I began to prepare the room for the birth at the hospital, he decided that he was going to leave and call him after it all was over. I maintained civilian medical insurance for her and Ernest, recognizing their need for it as recent graduates without a job, and planned to remove them from the policy as soon as they secured employment. I paid for a doula and a midwife, despite the presence of a doctor and my own licensure as a midwife and doula, as a precautionary measure. It was not a long labor, and when Isaac came into the world, he was as beautiful as Blake was.

When Bella discovered she was pregnant with Anya, Isiah was eighteen months old. Bella's husband received new orders and left for Germany before Anya was born. Bella gave birth quickly. When I arrived at the hospital before them, I prepared Bella's room with the lavender sheets and herbs in each corner of the sheets. As soon as Bella arrived and changed her clothes, her water broke, and she dilated to five centimeters. Within two hours, she was ready to push. The midwife instructed me to call the doctor because the baby was crowning. When no one answered, I went to the door and yelled for a nurse. By the time the doctor entered the room, the midwife had already delivered Anya. As soon as the midwife started preparing to cut the cord, I followed suit, and the nurses collected Anya and initiated her cleaning. When they laid her on Bella's chest, Anya raised her head. She was going to be an inquisitive one, I thought.

Soon after Ernest and Trudy were married, they announced they were two months pregnant, and seven months later Ella Francis was here. I asked Ernest and Trudy why they named Ella after Big Ma. Ernest responded, "Marie was never our grandmother." Big Ma was the grandmother who loved us unconditionally; we want her name to carry on. Ella will be aware of her legacy and take pride in carrying her name forward.

I explained to Trudy the steps I took to prepare for delivery, including hiring a midwife and doula who would work alongside your doctor throughout your pregnancy, be by your side during labor and delivery, and handle the situation if needed, just as I did for Bella. Trudy smiled and said yes, expressing her gratitude for the excellent care she received. "A midwife delivered me," Trudy said. Ella was born nine months after Anya. The beautiful baby cried a lot in the hospital, letting everyone know when she was hungry. Bella and Trudy decided to breastfeed. They both pumped their breast milk.

CHAPTER 29

....

Babies and Weddings

I CAN'T BELIEVE MY BABY IS HAVING BABIES. ALL OF MY CHILDREN, with the exception of Shauna, will bear offspring. Once Shauna began her menstrual cycle, I had her tubes tied due to her mental challenges and the presence of evil people in this world.

Lillian and Jacoby were driving to Virginia from Georgia. She would be staying until after the babies are born because Jacoby was directing a new movie in California. In the coming months, her due date would be too close for her to return to Georgia.

Three weeks ago, he asked for her hand in marriage and inquired about the possibility of holding a small wedding on the estate grounds. Jacoby has an old soul. He didn't believe in having a baby without being married to the mother. He believed in having a family structure. He expressed that he desired love in his life prior to starting a family, which he achieved, and he also deeply loved Lillian. Of course I responded yes.

Even though the country had reopened, we still took precautions. The virus continued to spread, resulting in numerous deaths. I asked Lillian if she was going to invite her father, and she replied no! I asked what were her colors; she said fuchsia, off white. I inquired about the members of Jacoby's family who were going to be present for the occasion. He mentioned his parents, his two siblings, their spouses, and his maternal and paternal grandparents. Lillian mentioned that she had discussed the invitation with Papa Jacque and Aunt Faye. She explained to them that Jacoby will hire a private jet to stop in Houston to pick them up.

Lillian and Jacoby should arrive in a few hours, and she can provide me with the necessary instructions. When she arrived, I knew she was going to be pretty big because she was carrying twins. She was carrying a boy and a girl, just like I did. I knew she was staying safe, but I told her don't allow everyone to touch your stomach, just as I told Bella, and Mama told me. "Everyone knew when she arrived," Mama" she screamed as she walked into the house. I was glad to see my baby girl. You know, the first place she went was the kitchen, because she knew Lois had her favorites there.

When they came in to sit and talk, I asked what she was going to name the babies, and Jacoby looked shocked. "I thought you didn't tell anyone," he said. "She didn't, I can tell," I replied, keeping our secret under wraps, uncertain if she felt comfortable sharing it with him.

It was a lovely day, and I wanted them to see where the wedding was going to take place. I explained that the wedding would be hidden by the trees, with a tent set up to prevent paparazzi from reporting any events. My staff is aware that only those who set up the tent and deliver the flowers will be outside. I have communicated with everyone involved, and we have ensured that everything is well planned. I asked Lillian who was giving her away, and she replied that "Papa Jacque and Pops" were escorting her down the aisle and giving her away.

When I asked Jacoby about the food, he mentioned a southern dinner consisting of chicken, barbecue, and seafood. I reminded him that our barbeque is not the same as what they prepare in Texas, given his family's origins there. I decided to roast a pig, serving half with North Carolina chopped barbecue and the other half with Texas pulled pork, both accompanied by various types of barbecue sauce. I asked Jacoby if any other family members would be attending, and he mentioned that his aunts and uncles from Georgia might be interested. Sure, but I need to know how many will be in attendance. They must take a COVID test 24 hours before entering the property; they won't need to book a hotel because I have plenty of space for them to stay.

I have five vacant four-bedroom houses. Lois and I will create a chart to determine the housing arrangements. My siblings and their families will be attending, along with my parents, Philip's brothers Donnell and Lamont and their families, and Aunt Faye and Jacque from Lake Charles. Jacoby's family will include his two siblings, their spouses, and their families, as well as his paternal and maternal grandparents, two uncles, and their respective spouses.

Later that night, we had the flower girls Anya and Ella try on their dresses; the ring barrier Isaiah try on his suit; and Blake, the bride's announcer, try on his. Everything fits perfectly. Trudy and Bella tried on their dresses, Trudy had to be altered a little, Bella's fit fine. I tried on my dress it was good, but when Lillian tried on her dress, I cried. The top was a cream color chiffon that draped off the shoulders, which gathered under the breast, and cream layered tool. It was beautiful.

Where did time go? It was the day before the wedding before we knew it. Jacoby, his parents, siblings, family, and grandparents, along with Aunt Faye and Jacque, arrived two days before the ceremony. The rest of the family arrived the day before, and that night, we had a cookout, with staff members preparing everything. My cousin Sean is a photographer, and I hired him and a couple of his staff to do the photos and the video; they too had to have COVID testing prior to entering the property. My brother Wiley provided music for the cookout, the wedding, and the reception. We had such a wonderful time. Jacoby presented his family, Lillian presented her family, and I extended a warm welcome to everyone in my home, hoping they would relish their stay. We planned to host the reception in the same location as our cookout.

On the wedding morning, I woke up at seven but remained in bed, reflecting on the day I married their father. It was the happiest day of my life because I loved Philip with all my heart and soul; now, I feel pity for him. How could he walk out on his children? I accepted that he no longer loved me, but the fact that he abandoned his children and had no contact with them bothered me. Over the years, our family expanded, adding grandchildren he had never met and two more on the verge of birth. His lack of interest prevented him from attending graduations or receiving wedding invitations. My grandchildren referred to my friend Joe as "Popa Joe" because they knew his name, but they were unaware of their grandfather Philip. The way Philip treated his own children as they grew up made his children distrustful of how he would treat his grandchildren.

I went out prior to getting dressed to check the decorations in the wedding tent and the reception hall. They were beautiful. Each chair on the isle was adorned with white lilies tied with fuchsia bows, while candles lined the altar on the stage. Along with the overtime my staff has put in, they each will receive a one-hundred-and-fifty-dollar bonus.

That morning, I went into Lillian's room; she was sitting up in her bed eating breakfast that Lois made for her, which consisted of all fruit. Pregnant, she consumed a variety of fruits such as grapes, watermelon, sweet peaches, and honeydews in the morning. We chatted and laughed, and I asked her, "How did she sleep? She replied like a baby, but I did get a visit last night. The ancestors told me they were proud of the woman I had become; how much they loved me, they told me to love on your man daily, and they knew the names the babies. They had nothing more to say.

This morning, Bella fixed my locks, so all I had to do was do my makeup, and Lois helped me with my dress. I went to check on Lillian and the bridesmaids; tears welled up in my eyes, but I could not cry because I did not want to redo my makeup. I checked up on the kids, and they were sitting like little angels. The wedding will start at seven that evening. The guests were to arrive at six forty at the tent, and we arrived at six fifty. All staff members who lived on the property and did not have any assignments were welcome to attend. We received a call from the front entrance, informing us that paparazzi were at the gate, asking questions, and that a drone was flying overhead, but the trees obscured their view. I proceeded to the front gate, requesting privacy and threatening to destroy the drone if it crossed my property line. The drone returned to its owner without any issues; my licensed guards will shoot it down with my permission.

Gerald, my baby boy, served as the official, while Jacoby, his father Lynell, and his brother Lynell Jr., his best men, entered from the right side of the tent. The procession started with Jacoby's maternal grandparents, then his paternal grandparents, and last was his mother Jennifer with a beautiful fuchsia one-strap gown. The procession then included Aunt Faye, who Ernest escorted, my mother Eliza, who Raymond escorted, and me, who Ernest and Raymond escorted. Trudy and Bella led the way, followed by Anya and Ella as flower girls, Isaiah serving as the ring bearer, and Blake announcing the bride's arrival. Both grandfathers dressed in tan suits, Lillian in off white, off-the-shoulder gown looked stunning. Eric Roberson's song "Lessons" was playing.

Tears streamed down my cheeks as I expressed gratitude to God for bestowing upon her a good man and for the ancestors' blessing of a wonderful life ahead of her. I looked over at Jennifer, and we both saw the happiness in our children, our youngest, our babies, who were about to have babies of their own. When they completed their vows, Jacoby took her face in his hands and kissed her so gently I knew she was in trustworthy hands. They jumped the broom; after all, photos were taken, and we partied with many of the staff members until after two in the morning. They decided to go on their honeymoon after the babies were born, but the staff had fixed up her room for a honeymoon suite. I let the staff know that we didn't need to report until noon, and we distributed the leftover food to every occupied house on the estate, including my own.

The passing of time is going by fast; I am in awe that Lillian has been married for five months and will be giving birth to twins in approximately one month. We had a Zoom baby shower, received all the gifts before the shower, and had a wonderful time. Jacoby would be returning today; he finished his movie and completed his ten-day quarantine to make sure he would not bring anything contagious to the house. Lillian had been on bedrest for about two weeks. Lillian decided that Jacoby, Fatima, her midwife, and I would be in the room during her delivery. I am certified midwife and doula, I felt that there should be someone else there, but I would have my say if I felt things were not progressing well.

I had explained to the doctor that due to their celebrity status, we required complete silence during the birth of the babies, and that we needed a secret entrance to enter and exit the hospital to avoid paparazzi. She understood and agreed. She had an appointment with her doctor and Jacoby today, and I was going with her. She had her bags packed for about two weeks, just in case. She consistently made the first morning appointment or the last one of the day. Today her appointment was at six, and I was glad Jacoby had arrived. When we arrived at the appointment, Dr. Lewis blushed when she first saw Jacoby. She asked the standard questions, lowered the bed for Lillian to sit on, had her lie down, and then raised the bed to perform the pelvic exam.

After the examination, she inquired whether Lillian was experiencing any pain, given that she had dilated to a four. I need you to go straight to the hospital because you may be giving birth tonight. Dr. Lewis made a call to the hospital, instructing them to dispatch three specific nurses, and requested security to meet us at the hospital's back entrance with a wheelchair. While on our way to the hospital, I called Fatima, the midwife, and told her we were on our way there. When we arrived, Lois got out and set up my chair, and security came out with the wheelchair.

Jacoby got Lillian safely in the wheelchair, and we all rolled in behind security while Lois went to park the truck. The nurses informed us of our room's location, and I proceeded to strip the bed, place the lavender fitted sheets on it, insert the herbs into the corners of the sheets, and then replace it with another lavender fitted sheet. I positioned the battery candles around the room and played soft Christian jazz. Dr. Lewis and the nurse arrived, taking her vitals and stating that she needed her water broken. Jacoby looks at me and says, "Ma," but I reassure him that everything is fine. Fatima enters after breaking Lillian's water and suggests that they get up and take a short walk. Jacoby, having hired private security, had blocked off a section of the hallway, preventing anyone from entering unless they wore a specific color armband. After three hours, labor pains were steady, and my baby knew how to breathe through her contractions. Fatima measured her dilation and found that she had progressed from four centimeters to seven by that point. Fatima said these babies are not playing; they are ready to get here. She refrained from lying down, as it would only prolong and intensify the labor, and she did not administer any pain medication.

They had a heart monitor on Lillian and a monitor checking the heart rate of the babies. We continued to feed Lillian ice chips, and she would sit on the large ball while Jacoby massaged her back and sides, which helped to calm her during her contractions. After four hours, Fatima checked to see how far Lillian had dilated, and she was at a ten. "Okay, Lillian, it's showtime," called Dr. Lewis. You can get in bed and deliver, or you can squat and deliver, depending on your preference. Lillian decided to squat on the side of the bed and help push out the babies; she would inhale just before a contraction, and during a contraction, she would push. We could see Baby A crowning, and within fifteen minutes at 2:37 a.m., at 6 lbs., 5 oz, 20 inches long, he was screaming his little head off. His name was Zachery Jacque Sessoms made his entrance before they could clean him off properly and lay him on her chest. At 2:40 a.m., Baby B arrived, weighing 6 lbs. 8 oz and measuring 19 inches in length. Zanna Charlotte Sessoms also arrived, and it was a competition to see who could scream the loudest.

Jacoby, Lillian, and I were in tears. They were beautiful babies. Jacoby's parents arrived while we were on our way to the hospital. Sharnell, the nurse, recorded the deliveries. Dr. Payne, Dr. Lewis's sister-in-law, was their pediatrician. After cleaning them, taking them to the nursery to recheck their vitals, applying their footprints to the hospital birth certificate, and placing an armband on them, they returned to Lillian's room. They each latch on, but Lillian realized she couldn't feed both babies simultaneously, so she asked the midwife if she could pump, to which the midwife agreed.

After I helped her to the bathroom for a thorough wash, she began pumping, while Jacoby took a nap. I took off the sheets, arranged some clean sheets of the same color on the bed, added herbs to the corners of the sheets, and layered another lavender sheet on top. As I waited, I called Lois and told her to come and get me. I went into prayer, thanking God for giving me the gifts from the ancestors, and thanked him for blessing me to be a part of five of my grandchildren's births.

CHAPTER 30

······························

Grandbabies

WORD HAD GOTTEN OUT THAT LILLIAN AND JACOBY WERE married, and Lillian had given birth to twins. Paparazzi gathered in front of our gate, eager to catch a glimpse of our adorable children. Jacoby and Lillian came to the decision that Lillian should stay with me, as he didn't want her to be in Atlanta for the next three projects he would be working on. They discussed the situation with me, and I agreed that Lillian would require assistance with both babies. Jacoby would work on a project for three months, then go into isolation for a week. He made sure he didn't contract COVID or anything else. Then he would come here for the next three months.

Lilian decided to get back to acting. The thought of being away from her babies for long periods made her decide being a mother was more important. Lillian decided to start working with Gerald in a financial company. She started managing the finances of Jacoby's projects, which proved to be a successful endeavor. Our pastor blessed the babies at six weeks, following the tradition of our ancestors blessing our children. I knew that someday I would be a grandmother, so I made twelve blankets, and I dyed each one of them blue, yellow, and purple for boys and pink, yellow, and purple for girls. When they dried, each one had their own design. After washing and drying them on the clothesline, I engraved their names on each one. I wrapped them in brown paper and tied the package with twine. Every time I had a baby, Big Ma would remind me that my blankets were unique, just like my children. Never compare one child to the other, as this can lead to resentment between you and them. They were beautiful. I had six grandchildren, three granddaughters, and three grandsons.

Lillian and Bella showed very little interest in the old ways. I asked their parents' permission to teach their daughters the old ways. My son Ernest and his wife Trudy had a daughter named Ella. When Ella began to speak, I observed that she would pronounce the names of her ancestors. Mama and Daddy came second, but I knew she was born with the gift. When Ella was about a year old, Trudy asked why she was using names she had never heard of, not Mama and Daddy. Ernest knew, but I had to sit down one night and explain it to her.

I began observing the distinct personalities in each of my grandchildren, with the girls in particular being very headstrong, protective, and bossy. Zanna was inquisitive. As a newborn, Zanna was always trying to hold her head up, see things, and look around to check out her surroundings. She was protective of Zachery. One day, I saw her take her pacifier out of her mouth and give it to Zachery to stop him from crying. She was a daddy's girl, and when Jacoby entered the room, she greeted him with a beaming smile. Zachery was a lot like me. He was quiet, observant, and a lap baby. Always wanted to be held.

Ernest, Gerald, and Raymond became surrogate fathers for Isaac and Anya, and when Jacoby became a part of the family, so did he. Bella, Shauna, and Lillian were surrogate mothers to Blake. Isaac and Blake were close in age, and they spent a lot of time together. They participated in a variety of activities together. They created a fort for themselves, where they frequently engaged in play. Anya and Ella were little divas who loved dressing up and getting attention.

Will they allow their children to learn French and Spanish?" I asked my children. They all said yes. Would they allow their children to learn to play a musical instrument? They were laughing. They all played the piano, and when we moved into the new house, there was a grand piano in the living room. Sometimes I would hear someone playing on the piano. They all sounded pretty good, according to what I heard. That was their choice, but by age four, they would all have swimming lessons and horseback riding lessons. Sometimes, I would see Raymond and Blake riding around the horse pen together. Blake loved it. When Isaac gets older, Raymond says that he is going to take him riding as well.

CHAPTER 31

. . . .

Understanding your blessing

MANY OF MY FAMILY MEMBERS HAD NEVER TRAVELED AND knew no world outside their neighborhood, city, or state. Along with educating them, I wanted them to experience a little bit of the world outside their community. Many of them had never flown before, and I wanted them to have that experience. My trip consisted of my close family, sister Carol, her daughter, Shay and both of her daughters, my three daughters, and numerous family members, some that I knew and others I was introduced too. I had two thirty-six passenger busses, that met me in New Orleans and Atlanta for transportation. If you can't do for your family, who can you do for?

Before Big Ma passed, she told me that I was the chosen one; I had to teach the women of our family what our gift was about. At our first workshop in New Orleans, I talked to them about how fortunate we were. There were very few families who could trace their family to Africa, but we could because of the stories Sarah told her children and the stories that had been passed down each generation.

We are children of God and God makes no mistakes. We have been labeled as root workers, hoodoo women, voodoo women and probably worse. In the years to come we will continue to be labeled with those names, or worse. We are healers, herbalist and we give thanks for our ancestors that have gone before us, who are still a part of us. Our ancestors are the reason we are here, they are the ones who paved the way. People say we worship our ancestors, which is not true. We talk about their strength it took to make the trip across the Atlantic Ocean, surviving slavery, being whipped, Jim Crow, and segregation. Our ancestors went through all of these things for us to exist in the world today. We don't worship our ancestors we honor them. We used roots and herbs to make medicine to cure illness.

Sarah learned from her elders in Africa. When she was forced from her homeland she practiced what she learned in secret and passed it down. Slaves didn't have access to doctors, so it was the slaves that took care of each other. Who do you think delivered the babies during those times? It was the midwives who used the same practices that had been taught in Africa. Practices that have been passed down for generations. How many of you were delivered by midwives? Quite of few raised their hands along with me. All my children were delivered in the hospital. Big Ma was a midwife and in the delivery room to make sure things were done right. During slavery those things were done in secret, at night out of fear.

We are strong women because Sarah and Minnie had to be strong to make the voyage from Africa to America. When they arrived in South Carolina they were stripped of their name, heritage, language, identity. Africans had to convert to the English language, being in a strange land and convert to their religious practices.

Voudou is an authentic religion, which came from West Africa during the slave trade. The meaning of the word means spirit or ancestors. Africans practiced their own religion, and worshipped God in their own way until their capture and came to the America's against their will. Their religion was looked as being evil, black magic. Hollywood movies destroyed the image of the Voudou religion by making it look like devil worshipping. Voudou and the proper term but the pronunciation of the word has been changed over time and the word was changed to Voodoo.

Many families turned away from their gift out of fear. Some family explained their gift as a mental illness. When some family members continued to practice their gift in secret when their family found out they were kicked out of their homes and banned from the family. They told other members of the family to stay away from them because they were evil. God made us in his own image. When the ancestors speak to us they are protecting us by warning us of danger.

First we needed to learn our history, our family needed to understand the hardship Sarah was faced with. When I first started my genealogy journey I found Sarah in the eighteen seventy censuses, she was eighty years old. I found her death certificate and it stated she died in 1880, and she was 90 years old, and she was seventeen when she gave birth to her first child.

With my calculations Sarah entered this country around 1805 and she was around fifteen years old.

Once she was on a plantation and when older African slave woman realized she had a gift, she was told never let the other slaves, the overseer, or master know, and she showed her the welts on her back. Sarah stayed to herself mostly and after a couple of years a male slave started to pay her some attention. The slave women on the plantation told her that the master felt it was time for her to start having babies, and he chose Lewis to breed with her because he too was African and by breeding them together they made stronger babies.

Lewis mother, Minnie, was pregnant when she arrived giving birth to him less than a week after arriving to the plantation. He was the only child she gave birth to because she refused to give birth to another child that was enslaved. Minnie constantly chewed cotton root, something she learned in Africa. Sarah feared the whip, so she allowed Lewis to move in her quarters and let him have his way with her. By the time she prepared to move to a new home she had seven children and was pregnant with the eighth child.

Harry Bercier was their new master, and he stated that he only wanted to buy a family, and money was not a problem. Sarah, Lewis, all of their children were not placed on the auction block, Harry Bercier wanted to go to the slave quarters to look at the slaves. When he saw Sarah he saw the kindness in her eyes, so he purchased her, Lewis, all seven children, and Lewis' mother Minnie.

The trip would be long and hard, but Bercier traveled with his slaves. He purchased three wagons, six mules, and he had his three of his men along for the trip. He was trusting of his slaves, he didn't use shackles. By having a family no one would try to run. Sarah took her medicine kit that she kept hidden in her quarters, she was given indigo by one of the slaves. Sarah and Minnie did all the cooking, and the trip took six weeks, but they finally made it. Bercier had about sixty slaves already and their family blended in with no problems.

Sarah and Minnie were cooks in the main house, Lewis took care of the livestock, the older children worked the fields, and the younger children stayed around the cook house where Minnie kept an eye on them. Our family remained on the Bercier farm after emancipation, becoming sharecroppers, picking cotton, and working the tobacco fields.

Bercier died in 1875. In his will Bercier divided his land between ten families that had been slaves for his family and our family was one of the families. Some of the families lost their land due to delinquent taxes. It was a family job to make sure that taxes were paid every year, we all chipped in to make sure that our legacy lived on. After emancipation, all of Bercier slaves stayed and worked as sharecroppers and they were allowed to build houses on the property they were willing to sharecrop on and he also allowed them to build a church that served as a school for the children during the day.

Many of the older children taught their parents how to write their names, and to read by using the bible. The first part of our trip we flew out to New Orleans, and we got there in time to load charter busses to go to Whitney Plantation. We had a private tour of the plantation where duties of the enslaved was explained. We learned how indigo was made. Once our tour was completed we returned to New Orleans, was given our hotel assignments. I had a conference room booked with food served for our first session. I had workbooks printed where it was easy for everyone, could write down notes, they could trace their genealogy back to one of the four daughters of Sarah. The book contained color photos of the different herbs that were used, and instructions on how they were grown, and photos of direct descendants of Sarah who are our ancestors. The older women passed down family information to the younger women.

Information that people didn't know I assisted with. Some information I had gathered from the ancestors before they passed and also using Ancestors.com by using the family tree I had posted, along with photos.

Day two of our New Orleans trip we went to Congo Square where we met with a young man who explained during slavery, the enslaved would come to Congo Square sing, dance, see relatives and practice their religion on Sunday. There were drummers and dancers and we watched their performance.

Like all the information that I have in my book all the medicine, herbs we used, stories told by the ancestors were stories that had been passed down for generations. After our tour we went to the mall to shop and eat. I had the conference room set up where we ate authentic New Orleans cuisine, but I had a car to pick up my cousin Shay, Bella, and I to take us to an authentic voudou shop where I purchased things that I wanted and after the owner explained how it is used.

Our review was short. We reviewed information we learned at the Whitney Plantation, what we learned at

Congo Square and the true meaning of Voudou that it was a religion that our ancestors was stripped of and had to be practiced in secrecy due to fear of being harmed by the white owners. It was also discussed how many blacks were Baptist, Catholics, and practiced other religions but also practiced voudou in secrecy because of the stigma that was placed on the religious practice. I reminded them to please be ready to board busses at four thirty in the morning because our flight would be leaving at seven and we had to be there two hours before our flight left at seven. I told them to take any leftover foods to their rooms and get up early enough to eat something because many of the shops in the airport would not be open and we didn't arrive in Atlanta until after nine, so at least they would not be famished when they arrived, because busses would be there waiting for us.

We would stop and eat once we arrived, and we would go and see where Martin and Coretta King were buried, and from there we would be on our way to Charleston S.C.

We arrived in Charleston around six that evening and we checked in our hotel, boarded the bus, and went out to eat the dinner at a restaurant in Charleston, which served authentic food. All the restaurants we ate at and the caterers we used were black during our whole trip. I believed in uplifting Black businesses, and I must say I have not been disappointed. The food we ate was delicious. The next morning we went to Gadsden's Wharf, where it was explained over one hundred thousand slaves entered here. I felt the spirit of Sarah when I arrived. It was a cloudy day, but when I stepped on Gadsden's Wharf the clouds separated and the sun smiled on my face. I thought I was the only one but others felt it too. A voice whispered to me and said "MY CHILDREN". We went to Gullah Island and learned some of their cultures, and that some of their dialog and why their language was dying out due to many of the young people leaving the island and not teaching the next generation.

I realized that many things of their culture many of us practiced.

We went to the slave market and many of us purchased items and when we returned to the hotel, we reviewed things we have learned that day and we had dinner catered for us in the conference room.

We left the next day on our way to Edgecombe County, North Carolina where we stayed in Rocky Mount N.C. We were all beat. So we took that Friday, and Saturday off. Sunday we went to our home church. Those that lived in N.C. had their cars bought to them, because our program will end Thursday and they will not be travelling back to Virginia.

Some had boyfriends and husbands meet them there and they had hotel rooms in the same hotel where they could get some loving they missed, but what shocked me was Joe and Jacoby drove down to meet Lillie and I. Bella told me to go that she had Shonda. I had not been away from Joe that long since we had started dating. I missed him but him being there made me realize how much I missed him.

Our last week, on Monday we went to a boutique where I had ordered white dresses, skirts, tops, pants, two head wraps, and everyone was given a purple cloth belt in many different sizes so that everyone had an all-white attire for our prayer chant on Thursday by the creek. When we returned we all went to the conference room where they were told to check their bag to make sure they had the attire they had chosen, a purple cloth belt, and two head wraps and when they finish checking their attire they needed to take out one head wrap. We practiced wrapping our head, it didn't matter how they wrapped their head, they chose how they wanted to wrap their head. We talked about practices that we had been doing for generations, but never knew where they came from:

Sprinkle salt under your door mat, keeping evil spirits out your house.

Women were not allowed at your house first on new year's day, and some of us didn't allow women at their house at all new year's day. A man has to cross your door sill first.

Between Christmas and new year you don't wash linen, towels, or washcloths.

Don't touch someone feet with a broom.

When the ancestors visited you in a dream, or when you are doing something that you know is wrong and you hear an ancestor, you are not crazy, they are warning you are making a bad decision.

Signs that was given, and everyone signs are different.

Everyone's gift was different.

We didn't choose this path, the ancestors chose us.

When we pay tribute to our ancestors, we pay tribute to life, not death.

I introduced to the African herb Imphepho. Imphepho was the sacred African herb that was used for various of things. On Tuesday we went to the family cemetery, and I asked what did they see different in the headstones? Shauna answered that some of the headstones were lavender, and that's when I told them that the ones with the lavender headstones were the direct descendants of Sarah.

I then showed them Sarah, Lewis, and Minnie's grave. I paid a service to keep the cemetery in very good condition, a fence around it because this was a way I preserved our family history. I gave each one two packages of Imphepho seeds. One package was to be used at the grave site and the other to be used in their private gardens. They were to spread a few seeds from the package on top of each ancestor that they had a direct connection to.

There were a lot of our ancestors out there and everyone needed to find their direct ancestor. Wednesday we did breakfast in the conference room, and I reviewed all the information we had received from New Orleans to Edgecombe County. I answered questions that needed to be answered and the rest of the day was a trip to the mall. I told them dinner would not be served and to make sure that everyone got their own dinner for that night and that Thursday we would have breakfast before we headed to our family homestead and there we would have a blessing ceremony for those who never had one. On Thursday morning we met in the in the conference room and we took a family photo and ate a nice breakfast and coffee before we boarded the bus.

When I sat on the bus Shauna asked me, "You nervous? No I replied. We are family. When we reached our family homestead we all gathered in the back yard and I was in the middle of the circle and we started singing, when I called to all those who never had a blessing ceremony middle of the circle and began to pray the prayer of blessing that Big

Ma had prayed over me, while the song "Lead me, guide me along the way" played in the background and those that knew the song sang with the music. I blessed at least thirty members of my family who never had the blessing ceremony and went through life confused about their gift and the dreams.

After the drummers started and we sang and danced. It was a beautiful ceremony, we returned to the hotel to rest and prepare for the banquet that we would be having to end our two-week exploration learning about our ancestors and the gift we all were given. At the banquet I showed a video of our trip. I gave them prayers to add to their book. Each one was given a necklace with a medallion, and I gave each one an opportunity to speak. I spoke:

The four principals of life according to Yoruba Spirituality

a. Have a relationship with God. Have your own spiritual connection with the God you serve.
b. Have a relationship with your ancestors, these are the people that came before you. They developed the culture and some of the ideas that you live in today. Say their names. The Europeans call them angels, the African culture call them ancestors
c. Have a good relationship with your parents and your family. d. We take care of our elders when they can't take care of themselves.
d. Have a good relationship with your community.

I reminded everyone their books are their private possessions, and they need to put them where no one else has access. If they need to purchase a safe let me know before they leave along with their address, and I will order one for them. On Friday we said our goodbyes to some, Saturday I said my goodbyes to others. I reminded them that this would not be our last gathering.

CHAPTER 32

Harry Bercier and Sarah, the connection

THERE WAS ALWAYS A CONNECTION BETWEEN NORTH CAROLINA and Louisiana. Many people thought Bercier was from Louisiana, where he had a sugar cane plantation with seventy-five slaves. But there was a weakness he had for slaves. No one knew his history, he never talked about it. Harry Bercier was the only child. Born and educated in France, he was the child of Mulattos who passed for white.

His father died when he was sixteen and his mother died two years later, he was left with enough money to last him a lifetime if he used it wisely. After taking care all of his parents affaires, he took the first ship to America, and settled in Louisiana. He bought a sugar cane plantation from a widow woman who was liquidating all her property so she could return north. He went to the slave auction, there he found about five families that belong to the woman he purchased his plantation, and after looking them over for scars, he purchased them. Each time there was a slave auction, Bercier never attended the auction. He spoke to the auctioneer and decided to inspect slaves prior to the auction because his interest was only to purchase slave families. When you purchased families you had less chance of runaways was a practice he wanted to experiment with. It worked. Many of the slave owners in his area had problems with runaway or rebellious slaves, due to inhumane treatment.

Not Bercier. Bercier parents were Haitian slaves, that were fathered by white slave masters or the overseer, and African slave women. They were runaway slaves that stored away on a ship leaving for France in the middle of the night to make a better life. Once the shipped docked in France the snuck away from the ship in the middle of the night. They lived off the streets until they found ways to earn an income like other Haitian mulattos. They finally found a place to live, and they worked hard providing for their son until their deaths.

He was taught his family history, his family also taught him to never tell anyone about his African heritage, not because it was shameful, but it was the only way to survive without being in bondage. Bercier developed a good relationship with many of his slaves, but there were some who did not trust him or any white man. The overseer knew before whipping any slave they had to have his permission, but he found other ways of punishment. The slaves took charge when it came to planting and harvesting sugar cane, the running of the main house and slave quarters. They knew if the harvest was a success, their plantation ran smoothly, meaning they had a happy owner. Furthermore they knew how their previous owner worked them from sunup to sundown seven days a week.

Five years had passed, Bercier had made a fortune with his sugar cane. Some of the men he associated with questioned when was he going to take a wife. They also informed him on how to have his white family and have a negro family. The practice was called placage.

Bercier attended a couple of the quadroon balls, but felt they were no different than a slave auction. The women were of mixed race. They were presented at a ball by their white fathers and black mothers, aunts, or grandmothers. The elder women would bargain, making deals with white men, that these women would be given homes, their children would be educated, and if there were son's they would be educated in France.

One day when he was at the market, he saw the most beautiful woman he had ever seen. He began to ask around who this woman was, and he was told her name. She was born in Haiti, an African mother, and a French father. Her family was part of a group of people called "Free people of color". Her name was Pleshette St James. One day he saw her out with an older woman, walked up and introduced himself to them. He would speak to her mother several times and ask could he come over to speak to her daughter, eventually he did. He courted Pleshette, for several months and he asked her mother for her hand in marriage. Eighteen months later they were married. Everyone talked about how beautiful their ceremony was and how nice the party was.

He loved Pleshette and she loved him. Fourteen months later she gave him his first son, Simon, and two years later she gave him another son, Adam. After the birth of Adam, Pleshette began to have a lot of physical problems. She had a rough pregnancy and hard labor. Pleshette could not feed Adam and bleed heavenly after giving birth. For months she continue to worsen, and when Adam was nine months old she died in her sleep. Bercier was devastated. He was hurt, and he mourned for a very long time after her death.

During his mourning he began to notice how his head maid Ariella looked so much like his late wife Pleshette. Not knowing his head maid was the half-sister of Pleshette. Their father had a plantation in Haiti, and in Louisiana. Before the Haitian revolution their father had returned to Louisiana never to return to Haiti. Their father Samuel recognized Pleshette and her mother one day while shopping in New Orleans, but he could not claim them because they were free. Pleshette and Ariella both had the same father, African mothers, they both were born slaves, but Haiti won their independence and slavery was still legal in America. Pleshette came to this country a free woman of color, and Ariella being born in this country made her a slave.

About two years after Pleshette's death Bercier began to bed Ariella, and after twenty years she had given birth to eight children. Bercier made it very clear to his sons Adam and Simon they were not to touch the daughters of Ariella. Adam and Simon were not stupid, they knew that Ariella was sleeping with their father, and too many people said that the children of Pleshette and the children of Ariella looked too much alike. After making numerous trips to North Carolina, checking on the house he had built, and harvesting cotton, he decided to continue harvest sugar and indigo in Louisiana, and cotton and tobacco in North Carolina. He traveled between the two states until the Civil

War began. Bercier decided stay in N.C. until after the war was over. He freed his slaves in N.C. and gave them an opportunity to stay on the land and work as sharecroppers or they could leave. When he returned to Louisiana all the former enslaved were still there except a few. Both Adam and Simon were killed in the war in Louisiana and were buried with their dear mother. The pain of seeing his whole family in the family cemetery was too much for Bercier, he had a heart attack and died a week later. The word reached North Carolina of Bercier's death.

Bercier lawyers in North Carolina went to Louisiana to meet with the lawyers in Louisiana so they could distribute all of his properties in his will. In his will he left his plantation in Louisiana to his four sons, and left money to his daughters by Ariella, and in North Carolina he left the house and fifty acres of land to Sarah and her husband Lewis. He left acres of land to other loyal former slaves. Arielle knew how to read and write, and she taught all of her children. In secret some of her children taught other slaves.

After the death of Bercier, Arielle and her children return to New Orleans, along with Sarah and Lewis youngest daughter Fannie. Fannie and Bercier son by Arielle, Frederick were married after the war. Sarah was hurt when she heard her baby was leaving the only place she knew. Sarah tried everything she knew to try to persuade Fannie from leaving but it didn't work. The day she left Sarah said one thing to Fannie, please come back before I die. After all of Bercier's affairs were settled, Bercier and Arielle had a son and daughter move from New Orleans and moved up North. Three of his sons continued to run the plantation, when Frederick was killed, leaving Fannie a widow with six children. After being gone for fifteen years, Fannie and her four youngest children moved to Edgecombe County, her two oldest went to college and moved to New York.

Fannie lived with her parents and took care of them until they died. Before Sarah died, she began to tell Fannie about her life in Africa. Sarah told Fannie the names of her parents, siblings, and the name of her village, but Fannie did not understand because many times Sarah spoke in her native tongue. She talked about her life before being captured, how she was blessed to see her children and grandchildren free from bondage. Sarah talked about how mean her first master and overseers were, that Bercier was a good master. One day during their conversation Fannie asked Sarah did she know why Bercier was a good master, Sarah said no, that's when Fannie revealed that Harry Bercier was a mulatto, a negro man.

CHAPTER 33

·····························

Choosing Love

OUR ELDERS ARE SLOWING UP AND YOU SEE CHANGES happening right in front of you.

Jacques and Aunt Faye are now ancestors, so we don't go to Lake Charles as often. I moved my parents into my house with me because they were getting older and needed someone to watch them daily. Pricilla is still one of my best friends, and she keeps me up on the family gossip. My children continue to stay in contact with their aunts, uncles, and cousins but not their father.

One night at dinner I asked my children why they won't give their father another chance, and Raymond replied, I was too young to remember the things he did when I was younger, I only remember the things that he did when I was older and that was nothing. Things that a father should teach me such as how to tie my shoes and a tie, you taught me mama. I tried to step in as a father figure for my siblings early in life when I saw everything you were trying to do. Mama there were many times I thought about not going to college or going to a local college so I could be here to help you. I tried to protect you mama when I saw him with Susanne, by not telling you. Philip does not deserve another chance, and I will not allow him to hurt me or my siblings ever again, if I learned anything from him is what a real father is not. I looked at him and said it's not your job to protect me, or your siblings, it's my job to protect y'all. I hoped I did a good job, and continue to do a good job, if not the ancestors will let me know.

I always told my children, everything glitter aint gold, and that includes choosing their mate. They may look good to you, but are they good for you? I've told them to surround themselves with good people, people who will encourage them to do what's right.

When choosing a mate there are some things they need to find out for themselves. Find out about their family. Never choose someone who is selfish, and only thinks about themselves. Never try to force a relationship to work. Never try to force your love on anyone. These things will eat away at your soul like acid.

When looking for love, find someone who is kind, someone who thinks of the best interest of others, someone who is willing to help others who are less fortunate, watch their family dynamics because that tells you a lot about the person. If their behavior is not like their family, give it time, usually that behavior will show in time. Love comes at different times. You may love them, but they may not love you at the same time nor will they love you in the same manner.

There is love in the air in my home. There will be two weddings in the spring. My son's Raymond and Gerald will be getting married. I knew Raymond had been seeing a young lady from Franklin who was a member of the horse-riding trail for about a year before Covid named Marie. Marie was a social worker in Franklin, and she has a daughter. They kept their relationship going through telephone calls, facetime, and zoom, during covid. When the country opened Marie and her daughter isolated themselves for two weeks, tested negative for covid and then moved on to the estate so they could be together. Marie had no family and grew up in the foster care system and all she ever wanted was a family. I always had a good feeling about her when she started to come around the family, and their marriage will take place in April. Marie's daughter is now my new granddaughter, and I will love her as I love my other grandchildren.

My youngest son, my Godly man, Gerald is marrying his high school sweetheart. After completing high school, Armonie moved to Texas with her parents and attended Prairieville State University and continued with her master's degree. Armonie has applied to law school at a local college in the area and they will be married in Houston in May.

Four of my children will be married by the end of the year.

Bella after praying over her at the blessing ceremony, I see a light in her eyes again, but she says before she gets involved again she needed to work on herself first. I see my girls have developed an herbal garden, and they are practicing the lessons that have been taught to them and they are teaching their girls.

Shonda has really shown her knowledge in her gift. On our trip she asked questions and if she still didn't have an understanding she would ask for more details. I always thought that Lois and my brother Wiley were seeing each other, but they kept their relationship secretive, for years. One night we were eating dinner, Wiley and Lois came in with a smile on their faces, and announced they were married earlier. We all jumped up and hugged and kissed them. They didn't want a wedding, they had been sneaking around for years. I asked why? Lois said she didn't know how I would feel about her and my brothers relationship. I told her she had been a part of the family for years.

After not being able to develop a relationship with the children, Philip married a woman he met on his job named Jessica and he decided to move back to Lake Charles to be closer to his siblings and ran the family farm.

I finally opened up to Joe expressing my love for him and explaining to him about my gift. He said he knew, without me even telling him. He knew a little about it from listening to his family years ago because his great aunt was also gifted. In order to love you I have to love all of you, and I see nothing bad you do with your gift. We had so much in common, he worked with me on many different projects, and he respected my opinion. Prior to covid he worked with me on the garden we developed on the property I owned across from the house. We planted apple, pear, and pecan trees. We developed a garden with tomatoes, cucumbers, corn, okra, cabbage, collards, lettuce, sweet and white potatoes, and strawberries. We taught high school students how to plant a garden and paid them hourly wages on weekends, and during the summer months, and gave them a bag of the fresh food we harvested weekly. During covid we had a smaller garden, but we harvested enough where we delivered food to our student workers twice a month along with other items and delivered it to their front doors. Prior to covid we had a masquerade debutante ball yearly, teaching young men and women from the poorer parts of town proper etiquette, and raising money for scholarships. Joe and I worked on many projects together, he not only respected my ideas and opinions, but we worked together to make improvements. We decided to get married in the Nassau, Bahamas. Before we married we went to counselling and I learned a lot about Joe's first marriage that he never discussed. I am sure that he learned a lot about my first marriage as well. We both wanted our second marriage to be successful and it took more than love to make a relationship to work.

One thing we realized was we were combining eleven adult children together, under different circumstances. His oldest daughter didn't want him to remarry, but his other children gave their blessings. Joe entered my life at a critical time and the lives of my children. My children never knew what love of a father was like until Joe came into their lives, now they are adults. Joe knew them from a very young age, but he was Mr. Dubois. He has been there for my children through some difficult times, he has shown them what a father is supposed to do.

I never tried to replace Joes deceased wife. I was there for his children just like I was there for my own. As we made plans for our wedding I realized that Philip and I never sat down and discussed our wedding plans, he just gave orders, and I made it happen. We both knew that some things in life could kill love and make you despised the person you once love.

We decided on the colors for our wedding, date, our wedding party, and the number of guests we would have. Once all the decisions were made, we hired a wedding planner. We decided to get married at the Margaritaville Beach Resort Nassau, Bahamas Thanksgiving weekend. Our wedding party will consist of family, my family party will be my three girls, Sabrina (Joe's daughter), my sister Carol, Pricilla (former sister-in-law and best friend), and Lois as my matron of honor. Joe's groomsmen were three of his army friends, his two sons, his brother Harry, and his oldest friend Otis is his best man.

Our colors are, men with tan linen suits, and white shirts, tan ties with tropical lavender boutonniere. My bridal party will wear a lavender gown, everyone's gown is different. Our four granddaughters will be our flower girls, wearing cute little lavender dresses with white sandals. Blake will announce the bride is coming, Isiah will pull Zachery in wagon as ring bearer also wore tan suits and white shirts. My sons will be ushers and my daughters in love will be my host wore the same as the ushers and bridesmaid's. There will be a white arch covered in tropical flowers, and tropical flowers on the end of chairs on the isle.

Our food will be catered by the resort, and people have the choice of seafood, chicken, or roasted pork island style. Joe, my wedding planner, our wedding party, our nanny's, family members, and I arrived five days before the wedding where we had a beautiful Thanksgiving. I wanted to get there to make sure no one would have any problems with their accommodation.

While there everyone stayed busy with the different activities like parasailing, horseback riding, fishing, massages, riding ATV's, shopping, and other activities that the island had to offer. The night before the wedding we had the wedding rehearsal dinner, after I went to my room and asked my children to meet me in my room after I soaked in the tub.

I explained to my children I was not having cold feet about my upcoming nuptials, but I wanted to hear if anyone had any doubts about Joe. I explained that Joe had signed a pre-nuptial agreement and if I died before him he had rights to live on the estate until his death, but he is not allowed to live with or bring another woman on our family estate, and he has nothing to do with the daily running of the estate or finances of the estate. We laughed and joked for a couple of hours.

Only Shauna stayed in the room with me that night. After everyone left for their rooms, we crawled in my bed, Shauna says mama whose bed I am going to get in now when it storms? I got you and if I am not there get in bed with Bella. Bella and I discussed it earlier. I finally fell asleep, and it was the most peaceful sleep.

That night the ancestors came to visit it was one of the best visits I had. Big Ma did all the talking. I was so glad to see and hear her voice. I had visits before, but only one other time from her.

She tells me how I have finally found the right one. He is kind, loving and very thoughtful. He works with you regardless of the situation. I am proud what you have done with the women of our family by teaching the right way to work with their Blessing. I love you Baby Girl. I slept peacefully with the ancestors watching over me.

My wedding was not until seven thirty that evening, so I rested all that day, around four that evening someone knocked on my door and it was my wedding planner. Sylvia, along with her were three other women. Have you rested? Yes I replied. The other women began to prepare a special bath for me once in the water these women began to scrub my body gently from head to toe. They assisted getting me out of the tub and oiled my skin until it had a natural shine from head to toe. The took me down to the bridal suite where my bridesmaids, and my flower girls were. It was around six in the evening. My bridesmaids was beautiful. When I entered the room Bella said let's hook these locks up and after finishing my hair, she placed tropical flowers. I don't like a lot of make up, I want to look natural.

It was almost seven and I was helped in my off- white gown. It was a strapless sweetheart neck with a see-through cape. At six fifty-five everyone was seated, my bridal party and I proceeded down to the wedding venue. At seven the procession started with the "That's the way I feel about you baby" the alternate version by the late Aretha Franklin. The curtain closed and it was my time to enter. I heard music playing and my youngest son walked over to me and said it's your time to shine. Mama you look beautiful. A song by the Temptations "This is my promise" played. Gerald escorted me to Ernest, and Ernest escorted me to Raymond.

My three daughters step away from the bridal party and join their brothers on each side of me. The minister asks who gives this woman to this man to join in holy matrimony, and they all say, "We do". The minister call for Joes children to join my children at the altar. They all made a circle around us, and the minister prayed a prayer of unity and love.

There was not a cloud in the sky, but big drops of rain would fall from the sky every couple of minutes. At one time I thought it was going to rain. The rain drops only fell on Joe and I. Our wedding and reception continued, and it was beautiful. We had the party of all parties. Days later when the DVD was delivered we all sat down to watch it, Joe mentioned the rain drops falling only on him and I. Shauna reply was "it was tears of the ancestors, blessing each of you and your marriage."

ASE'